ELEVATION: 6,040

ERNEST J. FINNEY

Texas Review Press
Huntsville, Texas

FIRST EDITION

Requests for permission to acknowledge material from this work should be sent to:

Permissions
Texas Review Press
English Department
Sam Houston State University
Huntsville, TX 77341-2146

Acknowledgements:
Two portions of *Elevation: 6,040* have been published in slightly different form as stories: "Sebastian's Son" in the Fall 2014 issue of *The Saranac Review*, and "Wolverines" in *California Northern*, Summer/Fall 2012.

Cover Design: Nancy Parsons
Author Photograph: N. X. Parke

Library of Congress Cataloging-in-Publication Data

Finney, Ernest J., author.
 Elevation: 6,040 / Ernest J. Finney. -- Edition: first.
  pages cm
  ISBN 978-1-68003-049-5 (pbk. : alk. paper)
 1. Rural teenagers--California--Sierra County--Fiction. 2. Mountaineering--California--Sierra County--Fiction. 3. Sierra County (Calif.)--Fiction. I. Title. II. Title: Elevation: six thousand forty.
  PS3556.I499E44 2015
  813'.54--dc23
                        2015018295

For
Barbara, Laura, Donald and Jimmy

CONTENTS

1981   1

The Jaunt   27

Sebastian's Son   57

Ophir Flat   79

Wolverines   93

About the Author   119

1981

Once the spring weather allowed, my mother always moved the family down from the ridge to one of the small towns close to Highway 49, so we could go to school, she told us, but we knew better. By Valentine's Day she was going nuts with cabin fever; it was like being locked in a room with a wild bird. She couldn't sit still, couldn't concentrate enough to read or sew on the treadle Singer. She'd pace, then stop and measure out the flour to make bread, then pick up a broom and sweep the floor, then pace again, twisting her ring around and around her finger. My sister and brother pretended not to watch her. We'd do our lessons fast to get outside.

You either belong in the mountains or you don't. Our place up on the spine of a Sierra ridge was high enough to guarantee us at least six feet of snow most winters. It was in the middle of a national forest of conifers and black oak on a hundred-twenty acre patented mining claim called the Empress of California that dated back to 1859. The nearest dirt road was four miles away; the nearest paved road was eight miles from that; the nearest town in winter, walking and skiing, was three hours down and nine and a half coming back up. No electricity, but we had running water from our spring. I was born on our place in 1969, before our cabin was built. We had a framed picture of us from *National Geographic Magazine*, taken by a visiting photographer back when the hippies were just beginning to take over the world. We lived in a yurt then, and in the photo my mother, in a long, stained white dress, her blond hair in tangles, a look of surprise on her face, was standing near the center pole, holding me in her arms as I nursed. My father in the background, his red hair in a nest of dreadlocks, bearded, shielding his face with his hand in the shadows of the white canvas flap near the entrance. Under the photo was a caption: In the California Sierra, a Young Family Lives Close to Nature. My father, Sebastian, belonged in the mountains.

Neither Sun nor Little would leave our work table before I was done. They were faster than I was. Nothing to do with paper and pencils came easy to me. We could hear Sebastian outside, splitting wood. It was like he was calling us each time the maul snapped a chunk off the pine round. Then a quick silence as he set himself for another stroke.

Our father had been an instructor in the Army, unarmed self-defense. He'd take on all three of us; we'd wrestle in the snow by the hour. We'd ski down our slope doing tricks, pretending we were in the Olympics, backwards, forwards, flips and jumps. We'd stack firewood. Build whole armies of snowmen and women. Drag broken-off oak branches near to the cabin to saw up. I was twelve that year, 1981; Little was ten, and Sun was nine.

"Roscoe, hurry up." My father had named me after a friend of his in the Army; he liked yelling my name, Roscoe this and Roscoe that. Our parents had an arrangement: my mother could name the girls and my father the boys; they planned to have ten children. My brother was named Elmer after my grandfather, so we called him Little Elmer, and then just Little. My mother had changed her name in college from Annette to Moonstar; she named my sister Sunflower. That was our family then.

When the weather finally would allow us to get out, my mother would check the for-rent section in the county paper and pick a town with a school where there was a house we could afford. Last summer had been a good one for dredging in the Yuba, and we had a pint mayonnaise jar almost a third full of flour gold and a pill bottle of matchhead nuggets plus a nugget the size of a radish. In March my mother got a ride down to Sacramento and sold the nugget to a collector and came back driving a five-year-old half-ton Ford pickup, and the house we lived in next, in Cold Springs, was the best we'd ever had: two bathrooms, and we each had a bedroom if we wanted. It came with a stove and refrigerator. We had stored our table and chairs and mattresses from last year in a friend's barn in Celestial Valley, but when we moved it all in, the house still looked empty. It was only fifty dollars a month; I tried to keep track of when it was due and things like that. Moonstar sometimes would forget. I was the oldest. It wasn't that I was pretending to be the man of the house because Sebastian wasn't there; I was just used to keeping my eyes open. Our father wouldn't leave the ridge under any circumstance, ever, so it was up to me.

School was always the same; it was like they had one idea for a student, and you had to be like that. Little was their model. He was what they were looking for. Sun was, too. There were elementary schools scattered all over because we were close to where three counties met—Sierra, Nevada and Yuba—so we could pick and choose, and we avoided schools we'd been to before: Sun said they were boring. We decided on a K through eight about a

3

mile from the new house. Our mother was dithering, enrolling us; that's what she called it in other people. It was just as well: she sometimes told too much: her high IQ, she was a UC graduate, and all the rest, and if the secretary was still listening, how she'd met her husband in Honolulu when he was on R and R; she'd been given the Hawaii trip by her grandmother as a graduation gift. We signed ourselves up: they were looking for students.

Little was in the fifth grade; Sun was in third grade. I talked my way into seventh. I had agreed to this school because there were enough kids that I wouldn't be in the same room as Little. The very first day, the very first hour, the teacher tested me for reading group. I was a slow reader. I liked words, and the different letters that made them up. Why was there such a big rush to gobble up the pages? The teachers always had a good reason. Moonstar was a speed reader. I didn't care what they called me. I read in low gear.

It takes a while to get the feel of a place. This one, Cold Springs, had been a sawmill town where logs were brought to be cut into boards, but now most of the mills were gone: the only signs of them left were the big three story tin burners that looked like Dutch windmills without the blades, where they'd burned all the scrap wood before chippers and particle board came in. Towns like this usually had a few big houses where the owners and managers lived, then a lot of smaller places for families and maybe a barracks for the single men. Some of the lumber mills had their own script money that you could cash in at the company store; we'd find the coins sometimes. The lumber industry was history by the time we got there. When a logging truck passed through town now, all conversation stopped and people turned to watch. There was one small sawmill left on the edge of town. A couple of grocery stores, and always a few bars. School, church, the post office and a lot of vacant buildings. A state maintenance yard. I heard some porchsitter tell another things were so bad Cold Springs couldn't even support a whorehouse anymore.

Elevation is everything in the foothills and mountains, because of the weather and because of the kind of people living there. Cold Springs, population 212, no doctors or dentists but also no serious snow, as Moonstar pointed out, was at 3,000 feet, compared to Nevada City, the nearest shopping town of any size, at 2,600 feet with 2,500 people. Or Sacramento, 400,000 people at 25 feet. It's just easier to live, lower down. My mother was raised next door to LA, the biggest city in the world. The kind of people living in Cold Springs were leftover folks, people who couldn't change, families that got stranded when the sawmills and the hardrock mines stopped paying. There was no work. Everyone who could find a job somewhere else left. The rest stayed until they got too old and couldn't take the winters anymore and then died in some rest home down below.

It was April first when a substitute teacher took over the third and fourth grade classroom. Their regular teacher had got into a bad accident on the black ice. The sub was 79 years old and walked with a cane, and everyone in the whole school was quiet, watching to see how long she'd last. At lunchtime I went home. Moonstar was still in bed. It took her longer and longer to rest up after her winter up in the cabin. She said it was the change in altitude. She had to adjust. I brought her a cup of coffee and got her awake. She just listened, and I went back to school. She must have phoned around, though, because she had an interview with the superintendent, and the next morning she was the new substitute teacher and Little and Sun and I called her Ms. McAdams.

Maybe in April the population of the town was 212, but by the 4th of July it was over a thousand. It

was like a different circus came through every day: a
yellow school bus painted green with a plastic head
on the front and a tail in back that made it a dragon;
red Volkswagens spotted like ladybugs; vans with
murals; bread trucks with curtains at the windows
and stovepipes coming out the roofs, piled with
lashed-on duffel bags and bundles; regular pickups
loaded with hitchhikers in the back.

We had been watching this summer migration,
as my mother called it, for as long as I could remember.
Once it got warm the hillsides filled up with people,
sort of like the redbud or dogwood or Scotch broom
that surprised you by suddenly flowering all over
the place. The spectacle was worth observing: you
never knew what you'd see. A Mercedes pulled up
in front of the store. The driver got out first, wearing
leather clothes and a coonskin cap and carrying a
muzzle loader, just like Daniel Boone, Little said.
Out of the back popped five women in blue United
Airlines uniforms. The man had money; he bought
a big house that belonged to the family that used
to own the bank. The town kids lined up to do
errands for him: he was loaded. A swami started a
commune and retreat and a Tibetan started a second
one. Motorcycle gangs. Poets and artists. Actors and
actresses. Veterans in old camouflage jackets. And
more than plenty of students, probably the largest
group of newcomers, my mother thought, all dressed
like hippies from the sixties. Long dresses and bib
overalls, bangles and rings on every toe and finger.
I kept an eye out for the girls that didn't wear bras.

There were three bars close by, two that served
food and one that rented rooms. Most of the newcomers lived in the neighboring Forest Service camp-
grounds or rented shacks. From the house we lived
in we could hear the carrying on for hours after
sundown. Shots, yelling, motorcycles roaring, sirens,
more shots. In the daytime the mountains and forests
seemed to absorb the newcomers.

*   *   *

Sitting on the porch of our Cold Springs house, Sun and I would reminisce of an evening about the time when Little was gone, mostly about the worst situations, to keep it interesting. Little liked those stories; he'd encourage us. "Then what happened, Sun?"

"You remember what Sebastian always says to do if you want to disable someone: use your boot; kick him in the kneecap? That's what Roscoe did. The guy let go of me in a minute. But his wife pulled out a machete."

"All over some beer cans?"

"That campground dumpster was always our dumpster, and we had a perfect right to all the aluminum cans in it. That's the only money we had coming in that spring. I don't think Daddy even got the dredge in the river; it never stopped raining. The water was too high."

Little had missed a whole seventeen months of excitement. He'd woken me up by moaning one night; we slept in the same bed. We were living in a place about six miles from here then, Blue Canyon, population 38. I woke up Moonstar. She took Little into her bed and I went back to sleep. I went to school the next morning but Mother kept Little home. At noon Little was moaning louder and had a fever of 102. That night he was worse. Every time she touched the lower side of his stomach he'd scream. It was hard to tell when my mother got excited, she didn't get loud or swear, but she forgot things. She forgot not to flood the carburetor and wore the battery down trying to start the car; it was a '68 Chevy Nova then. For the county ambulance you had to pay 150 dollars cash before you got a ride. She phoned Grandmother, and three and a half hours later my grandparents were knocking on the door. They tried the hospital in Nevada City, but the emergency room doctor was out and didn't answer his phone. My grandparents ended up driving Little all the way home to the hospital in Sunnyvale. By that time Little's appendix had burst and he was nearly dead. Grandmother phoned the next day and then three days later to tell us he was out of danger. It was agreed they'd keep Little until he got better. But then Grandfather wouldn't give Little back after he was well. Hung up on Moonstar when she tried to reason with him. After a year, I thought we'd never see Little again.

"Roscoe, remember the time we got the cheese?" The county had dumped a ton of pasteurized cheese in the campground, forty-pound cardboard boxes full of these two pound orange bricks, along with ten pound sacks of elbow pasta. "It was so good. We had macaroni and cheese for the next month." Sun was cracking up, remembering, hardly able to speak. We'd cooked it on the Coleman stove in the tent. We couldn't afford to rent even a trailer that time, much less a house. All of us in the campground had the stuff for breakfast, lunch and dinner.

What I remembered best about that particular time was Sun and Moonstar yelling over to our neighbors, "You disgusting degenerates." Sun was just a little kid, but she was as loud as Moonstar. At night when our neighbors' lantern was lit you could see through our nylon tent wall into theirs, and they thought it was funny to put on a shadow show for us if they thought we were watching. Sinister characters, my mother called them. Dope dealers, crack and meth. By that time you could get pot anywhere; the foothills were full of marijuana grows. A kid told me there was even a pimp in that campground with a string of three girls he sold to the wannabe hippies. We moved our tent in the dark that night to the only open space, next to the overflowing toilets. Moved in the rain the next morning, out of the campground into the forest. I'd always thought that trees were like a filter that would protect you, but during the storm that struck later that day a madrone branch came down and smashed the front of our tent. The tree drove us back to the campground and we spent the night in the toilet.

Little had been back with us five months. I couldn't decide if he'd been different like this before his appendix was taken out or if this was something new. He liked to sit alone holding a Bible now on a Sunday. He also like watching TV whenever he could sneak a look at someone's set. We had never owned one, not just because we didn't have electricity at the cabin but because our mother thought TV was a waste of time; idiot boxes, she called them. In Sunnyvale he had been in an advanced class where he learned Spanish and Algebra and they went on field trips to all the museums in San Francisco and LA. And he had an expensive camera now, and could develop film, just like Grandfather. And he knew how to talk back better than I remembered, especially to Moonstar, and got a few slaps for his trouble.

When I asked Moonstar when Big Elmer and Grandmother were coming up, she pretended she didn't hear me. They came every summer for two weeks, never missed. Stayed at a lodge or in their RV. Hiked up the dirt road to see Sebastian; he wouldn't leave the ridge, even for them. I knew there had been a scene when Moonstar went down to get Little back. Little didn't want to talk about it. It had always been hot and cold with Moonstar and our father's folks. With Big Elmer, really. Right before I was born, the story went, Moonstar's mother phoned Grandmother and said Sebastian had ruined her daughter's life. We had never met Moonstar's family.

If Little had changed, so had Moonstar. Here in Cold Springs, even after the school closed in June, she had friends, people who came over to the house and visited, drank chamomile tea with her. Teachers. Like

9

a club. Once I heard Moonstar laughing, a long long laugh. Had I ever heard her laugh like that before? I didn't think so. It started out a summer to remember. We didn't go back up to the ridge. We stayed in Cold Springs because Moonstar was teaching a summer class in remedial math and working in the office on grants two days a week.

It was the end of July. Little and I were sleeping in the screened side porch of the house, for the breeze. We were both tired out because we were making money loading mill ends for Mr. Carter. Little didn't snore but he kind of whistled when he exhaled. And he sweated when he slept; his skin would be as hot as a stove top, and slippery. We slept in our jockey shorts with just a sheet over us. The foothill towns could get hot in the summer; it had been over a hundred that day. Little slept heavy. I didn't know where he went when he closed his eyes but it wasn't in this world. I slept light and was ready to go the minute I opened my eyes.

I heard the pads first against the wooden floor of the front porch. I thought it probably was a raccoon or a possum. Then the stupid animal knocked over a shovel leaning against the wall and I made myself ignore the sound, kept my eyes closed. Noises in the night weren't always bad if you didn't allow them to be. There was a long long silence. Then an animal sound I'd never heard before, as if something was caught and was trying to get away as it rolled across the porch thrashing and squealing. You have to wait and listen to understand the dark, my father said. So I didn't try and look. I waited.

Grunting, squeaks and more grunting. I knew then: it was a pair of porcupines mating on the porch. Sebastian had told us there was a code in the mountains that porcupines were protected, because they were so easy to kill that if you were lost you could knock one in the head and get a meal. Not that anyone in their right mind would mess with a porcupine's quills. But outside that, the animal was considered a general nuisance. They would come around the cabin and chew up our work gloves for the salt, or take a nibble out of a shovel handle. I listened. They were a lusty pair, these porcupines, rolling down the length of the twenty-foot porch and then coming back again. My mother said you could tell a lot about the soul of a mammal by what occurs during mating. I had never given porcupines much thought before. At the cabin my father would get up and swat the porcupines away, chase them off the property with a broom. Knock them out of our fruit trees because they'd kill a young apple by eating the tender new branches. Dogs impale themselves on the quills when they try to worry a porcupine, and it's hard work on everyone to pull the quills out with a pair of pliers. They don't come out easy because there's little barbs on the pointy ends of the quill, and you have to get them out or they'll fester. I'd found foxes and martens starved to death, their mouths nailed shut with quills. Some people shot porcupines on sight to spare the dogs.

These two were still going at it like they were having the time of their lives. I didn't begrudge them their fun, but the grunts, groans and squeaks were getting too loud. I was thinking it over, encouraging myself to get up and get a broom and drive them away because the neighbors might not be so kind.

I raised up to take a look first. In the light from the half moon I could see the shapes of the porcupines. I watched as they rolled down the porch, then came back toward me. I could see the outline of one of the porcupines, but I couldn't understand what I was seeing of the other. Porcupines can go thirty pounds easy, but this one was bigger. Then, watching and watching more, I understood there was only one porcupine; the other was our thick heavy doormat the porcupine was rolling around with. When I realized that, I heard myself yell, "You stop that now." The sound of my voice froze the porcupine where he was, holding the hairy mat on top of him. As I watched he let go of the mat with a squeak and waddled off. I went back to sleep.

We were up early, waiting by the road for Mr. Carter to pick us up with his flatbed and trailer. This morning we were going to load more mill ends, two-by-tens about three feet long. And we couldn't just throw the boards on any which way: we had to stack them like we were putting dominoes back inside the box. Mr. Carter, a former millwright, wore bib overalls and had a beard and a cheekful of Red Rooster, but he said he'd dressed like that years before he ever saw a hippie, way before the sixties, when his grandfather had lived there. Sebastian had a longer beard and red dreadlocks down his back, and wore blue coveralls with a wool sweater on top and a pair of yellow knee-high rubber boots. My mother asked me if I wanted the same kind of shop coveralls too — she had to order them from a catalog — and I said no thanks. I was going to look like everyone else if I could.

Mr. Carter lived in a house built of these same mill ends, nailed together in a pattern called a running bond, like with bricks. It was kind of ingenious, the way they made up the ten-foot-high outside walls. There were windows too and a regular gabled roof with a front door. The inside walls were made with studs and sheet rock. He had us smear linseed oil over the outer walls, and they looked fine. People were always stopping to take a picture. He had a wife and a couple of granddaughters.

Mr. Carter had a deal with the sawmill that he'd haul the scrap wood away; they didn't have a chipper, and the big burners had been outlawed by then. He paid me a dollar and Little 50 cents an hour, plus a generous lunch. He was building ten-by-thirty-foot one-room cabins on his property by the river. Tourists with money were beginning to show up along with the usual hippies and needed a place to stay.

When I told Little about the porcupine and our doormat, he listened but I could tell he didn't believe me very much, though he was too polite now to say that. When we got home I showed Little the doormat, picked it up by the corner like a dead animal. When I gave the mat a slap against the porch rail, a lot of quills flew out like darts.

Little said he was going to stay awake, but he was whistling before his head hit the pillow. I waited and waited and fell asleep myself until the noise I'd heard the night before woke me up. I watched that porcupine a while before waking up Little. The animal was doing the same thing, quills scraping against the wood porch like a straw broom sweeping up broken glass.

You could never be certain that Little was awake when he said he was so I gave him a good pinch on his right earlobe to make sure. We both watched the animal roll back and forth the length of the porch until he got tired out and ambled off into the dark. Neither of us could sleep right away.

"Why does he do that?" Little wanted to know.

"He thinks the door mat is a female porcupine."

"Couldn't he just be playing?"

"I don't think so: don't you see he's in love with the mat? He's mating."

We got up; neither of us could go back to sleep. Turned the porch light on. We spent some time examining the mat. No one in the family used the front door to get into the house: I pointed that out to Little, but even I understood it couldn't make any difference to the porcupine. The quills were about six inches long, the color of a drinking straw but much thinner. We could ask our father about this, but not our mother, who would have at least five different answers and would just confuse the issue.

The next day was Sunday, and neither Mr. Carter nor Little worked on the Sabbath. Little was the religious one in the family; he caught that from Grandmother, who was a believer. She told me once, "What have you lost in the long run, if you believe in something good that turns out not to be true? I loved my grandmother, but I would have liked to say, "A lot of time and money, if those groups up here on the ridge are an example of religion." It wasn't the only change in my brother: it was almost like a few of his original parts were different, like his right arm had been exchanged for someone else's and that was why he could throw a baseball better now than anyone else in school. After breakfast Little sat by himself with his Bible. He never opened it; I'd stopped making comments. We all stayed quiet for about the ten minutes he took. I didn't think he was praying, but I never asked. Moonstar offered to take him to church but he always shook his head no. There were enough churches around now; you couldn't count them: Catholic and a couple different kinds of Protestant, the Tibetan and the Swami at the ashram and more.

We both stayed up the next night to watch. Along came the porcupine, and he grabbed hold of the mat, making all his noises and rolling up and down the porch. That animal wasn't playing. I speculated to Little that maybe it wasn't so easy to mate with another porcupine because of the quills, and this fellow fell for the mat because he didn't like getting stuck.

Little made no comment but pulled out his camera and took some pictures. The flashes didn't even slow down the porcupine; he grunted louder, in fact. The porcupine finally wandered off, leaving a lot of nearby dogs barking. The next night was the same story. And the next night too. Little was waking me up to watch, now. He named the porcupine, in fact: Peter Paul. He took more photos. The visits went on for a couple of weeks.

We moved to another house in Cold Springs right before school started. Moonstar had got into an argument with the landlord; she'd come into the house red-faced and told us, "Pack." I was sorry we moved. The new place was situated on a dead-end street in a cluster of other houses and sheds bunched together on a half acre of land that sloped uphill. There were a dozen apple trees, leaning uphill too to stay on the incline. Each one of those trees had uniform peck marks around the trunks every square inch, like a machine had done the work instead of the woodpeckers. The street was blacktopped. There was a crisscross of telephone and electrical lines strung from poles with lights on top that went on when it got dark. Too many houses and too many people.

Some other renter had left an old electric stove out front where the lawn used to be, and a '63 Taurus was up on blocks on the street. The metal roof of the house was rusted orange and when the dark shingled walls lit up outside as the sun went down it looked like the place was aflame. Clumps of lupine and poppies were still flowering among the dried out weeds out back on the slope. People joked that to live around there you had to have one leg shorter than the other.

Beyond the houses, a lot of brush maple, wild lilac and manzanita. Beyond that, the forest, mostly conifers. It went forever, miles and miles of green. If you walked far enough in, you'd start to see the old stumps where sections had been logged off, two or three times since the Gold Rush, Sebastian told me. In just the right place, at just the right moment in a certain morning light, I could see where two ridges overlapped. Then, just for an instant, I'd see our ridge.

Picture our cabin and Sebastian sitting out on the
chopping block smoking his Sherlock Holmes pipe,
putting an edge on the splitting ax with a flat file.
There was no way to calculate how much I missed
that ridge. 6,040 feet.

Peter Paul was not a fussy eater. We'd give him
windfalls, split the apples open and sprinkle some
salt over them. We'd kept him secret from Moonstar,
moved him to the new place in the washtub Little
had dropped over him, covered up with a sack.
There was an old poultry run out back, and we put
him inside the chicken house. We didn't know what
he might do, like shoot his quills into our faces or
even bite us, but he was mostly docile, his beady eyes
watching our every move when we got close.

Peter Paul usually sat there like a lump until by
chance one evening Sun threw a green tennis ball at
him and that got him going. He played with that hairy
ball like a kitten would, teasing it until it squirted out
of his grasp, then chasing after it. The best was when
he'd get on his back and hold the ball up to his eyes,
turning it around and around. It was mostly at dark
that he'd get moving into first gear, up and down the
dirt run. He liked the apples and would lap up water
from his dish. Sometimes we put the front door mat
inside the chicken run and Peter Paul would come
alive then, tussling in the dirt, rolling over and over,
flipping the mat in the air. We could watch by the
hour, sitting on our heels in the moonlight.

When Moonstar found out she said we could
keep the animal if we took care of it. Peter Paul was
popular for a while; kids came over, and some adults
too, for a look. I pretended not to be worried when a
neighbor lady said, "I know what I'd do with it. Kill
it before the dogs get at the thing." Little pointed out
that P and P was our pet. The big fat woman didn't
like the answer and said something under her breath.
She was the school bus driver and a second generation
resident and owned her own mobile home, but now

that our mother was a teacher she had to keep her opinions to herself. Moonstar had signed a contract for the school year. I hadn't caught on yet that it meant we weren't going back to the ridge.

After we started school we didn't have a lot of time to spend with P and P. We'd sometimes forget and leave the door open to the run, but the porcupine never left. Or we'd forget to feed the thing; we had a fifty pound bag of dog food by then because the apples were mostly gone, eaten by the deer who passed through at night. We only allowed P and P to have the mat on Friday after school. The doormat had taken a terrible beating and was falling apart. It had unraveled some places into long strands of rope.

I invited kids from my eighth grade class over to see the porcupine. I'd get a shovel and flip him over on his back and we'd watch him wiggle himself onto his feet again. Or I'd tease him, taking the mat away. Both Sun and Little would yell at me, "Knock it off, Roscoe. You're a nitwit, Roscoe. Quit playing the fool." That last was what my mother always said.

All those tales people like to believe about taming wildlife—that P and P would come when called or follow us around like a pet or eat out of our hands—were false. He was like any other wild animal; he had his own habits. Which were mostly eating, sleeping and screwing the mat.

When *The Mountain Messenger* printed one of Little's photographs of P and P wearing a red ribbon for his birthday, sitting on a bucket begging, a few people wrote letters to the paper telling their own animal stories: a Steller's jay who would peck at the window when the dog's dish of food was empty, visits from bears, a cougar asleep on a front porch swing. Sun's fourth grade class walked over from school to take a look.

*   *   *

I could have hiked over to the cabin. Take all the shortcuts, leave early, five a.m., get there before dark. Spend what was left of Saturday and come down Sunday, be back by noon. A day didn't go by without me thinking of Sebastian. The whole family had stopped even talking about him, I noticed. But I didn't walk over, not the whole summer or the fall. I knew he'd never leave the ridge. He'd get supplies from Mr. Elliott, the watchman at the Upper Seven Aces mine, who came in to town once in while during the summer.

It dawned on me in October when the heavy rains started that we weren't going to winter at the cabin because of Moonstar's contract with the school district. We were going to stay right where we were. I guess I'd believed we'd leave Cold Springs: we always went back to the ridge, no matter what. Like that year when Little was gone: like always, we stored our things and went out to the state road to hitchhike closer to our ridge. It was a Saturday, and the day had begun with the sun in the sky but by noon it started to drizzle, then rain. We stood by the side of the road, the treads on the tires of cars going by whipping water over our legs. Local teenagers drove by honking, yelling, some throwing their empty beer cans our way. We weren't the only ones standing out by the road. There was a young couple with a dog on a leash and a red rooster in a cage, two brothers with the longest beards I'd ever seen, and a girl with a baby. The cars slowed down to look at the girl. One stopped, full of local boys. Moonstar whispered, "Don't go; don't go with them," but the girl got in anyway. Mother thought she could tell good vibes from bad before she got into a car. In the sixties she'd refused plenty of rides; that was before she had us kids. She told stories about when she hitched all over the USA, Mexico, Canada and western Europe.

No one picked us up, not the next morning either. We'd slept in an abandoned car. I remember standing next to Sun, soaked through, waiting. Moonstar told Sun, "Hold Roscoe's hand; we don't look pitiful enough to get a ride." That did it: an hour later we were on our way in a logging truck that got us close enough to start walking to the ridge and the cabin. We always went back.

No matter how many times I try to remember, I can't work out how it was I started sniffing gas and huffing glue. The why. I knew better. I was over a kid's house; he was in my class. Down at Cold Springs there was always a lot of fuel around, cans of it for chainsaws and generators: we kept a five gallon can for our truck because the gas station was never open when you needed it. The six of us were taking turns throwing a knife against the board and batten wall of a shed in the backyard. In our family we never thought to play with knives: they were tools, something you skinned and butchered with.

One of the older kids went into the shed and came out with a five gallon Jeep can. While we watched he unscrewed the cap and put his face to the opening and took a long sniff through his nose. "Wow." He fell to his knees, yelling, "I'm high, I'm high." I took a turn. Fitted my nose and mouth to the opening and inhaled as long as I could. Nothing. The can was on a low stump, so I was bent over. I went to straighten up and kept going over backwards into the weeds. It was like someone had taken a toilet plunger to my face and sucked out my tongue, lips, nose, eyeballs and brain. And worse, I vomited up white mucus. No one else did.

I wobbled home and was sick again. Moonstar said it must be the flu and made me some vegetable soup. Next day I recovered but the same thing happened when I sniffed again. The higher octane grades like Supreme would send me further and faster. Then huffing. A long worm of airplane glue into a plastic bag was quicker than gas, but I had headaches for days later. I never got much out of aerosol cans.

Me and my friends started skipping school. One kid's older brother would take his mother's pickup and we'd drive down to Sacramento where no one knew us to buy glue for our model airplane club. I had my own gallon of gas now and kept it in the chicken house. When I needed a lift I'd go out to look at P and P and have myself a sniff.

Sun must have been throwing the green tennis ball for the porcupine, I never saw her as I wandered past, but she saw me and yelled, "What are you doing, Roscoe?" I don't think I understood the question, lifting my face from the gas can. I was going to say something soothing but I spit up my breakfast when I opened my mouth. "I'm telling," she yelled.

Moonstar, Little and Sun were all standing in the kitchen waiting when I came in the house. My mother started out reasonable. "Roscoe, sit down; I'd like to talk to you." I sat down at the table with my brother, sister and mother. It was an old kitchen: it had a pantry and wainscoting halfway up the twelve-foot walls. I could see through the open window to the sweep of forest on the ridge across from us. There was a stand of madrone trees on the slope because we were only at 3,000 feet. Good firewood. Orange bark peeled back on the trunks like the skin on a peach. They didn't grow up at the cabin on the ridge. Too high: elevation is really important in the mountains. I thought I was going to be sick again.

"Roscoe."
"Roscoe."
"Roscoe." They took turns.

Moonstar: "I'm surprised at you, Roscoe. Do you realize that by sniffing gas you're burning up your brain cells? Destroying yourself? Turning yourself into a vegetable?" I made no comment.

Sun: "You have to stop hanging around those punks."

Little put me in the cross hairs of his camera and I tried to swat the camera away but missed and got sick instead.

It was three weeks until Thanksgiving. I stayed home from school, stayed in bed sometimes. When I went outside I'd get dizzy. I'd throw the ball for P and P, who still liked the game. He made me smile: it was like watching a cactus waddle. I tried to read but got headaches. I noticed all the gas, glue and kitchen aerosol cans were gone. When everyone came home it was like I wasn't there. They'd talk about me. "Maybe he should go to rehab." "Look how thin he is." "Addictive personalities can't help themselves." "My science teacher thinks huffing glue is worse than heroin addiction."

I convinced everyone I'd stopped, and I went back to school. Both Little and Sun kept an eye on me. I was never alone, to and from school. At recess and lunch, one of them was around too. I was feeling okay, not wonderful but okay. I was outside one afternoon, watching Little and Sun play ball with Peter Paul—Moonstar was at the school at a meeting—when three town dogs ran into the yard and got into the chicken run and went for Peter Paul. Little and Sun started yelling and throwing rocks at them. I had to close my eyes; I couldn't watch. I knew what would happen.

The neighbors tried to get Moonstar to pay the vet's bills. One of the dogs had to be put down. One lost an eye. Moonstar got free legal advice from the school district. Their attorney wrote the neighbors that the dogs were unlicensed, were in violation of the leash law, and were trespassing when they tried to kill the family pet.

Then Mr. Gable, the state game warden, showed

up at the house on a Sunday. I remembered him coming to whatever school we were at every year to talk about the wildlife in the Sierras. He knew the mountains. He was a fly fisherman and always gave us a demonstration, did the back and forth with the rod, whipping thirty feet of line out to place the hook in a bucket. He showed us how to tie flies. He was wrong to worry that the town people were jacking deer. They were too lazy to go out anymore at night with a spotlight. They had all the cheese they could eat. The game warden had received a formal complaint that Moonstar was keeping captive an animal on the endangered species list.

When he saw it was a porcupine he just laughed. Flipped Peter Paul over and examined the animal. "You got the right name for him; he's a male of the species. Nocturnal. They like to roam at night." He pointed out that it had four toes on its front feet and five toes on its back feet, something we already knew, and thirty thousand quills, something we didn't. "Let's count them," he said. He was funny. Little got the warden a cup of coffee, and he watched awhile as P and P waddled after the green tennis ball. He wanted our mother to phone him when she got home.

When Moonstar came home we had a family meeting. Moonstar said maybe it was better to free P and P in the forest, let him return to the wild. We all looked at each other, until Sun said she thought it was a good idea. The game warden came the next Monday morning and took P and P away in a gray plastic carrier. I couldn't tell if it was Sun who was sniffling or Little.

That afternoon I was walking home alone from school because Sun and Little had orchestra practice, when a kid I half knew from another school and his older cousin stopped to give me a ride. They had a six pack of beer and I drank one, then another. We drove the thirty miles to town and got more beer and picked up another kid I'd never met before. I don't remember what happened after that.

A lot of people asked me about the accident, but I didn't remember anything. The investigator from the Highway Patrol visited me five times in the hospital and talked about the skid marks, how many times the car rolled, the blood alcohol content, the estimated speed. The other three boys died. I was lucky, everyone said, with just a broken collarbone and arm and internal injuries, plus the cuts when I went through the windshield and was thrown clear. I stayed in the hospital seven days. I knew I was too far behind everyone in my class to ever catch up.

Every afternoon Moonstar and my brother and sister visited me. Both Sun and Little interrupted each other telling me the latest on Peter Paul. Four days after the porcupine was taken away there was a scratch on the back door: it was P and P wanting his breakfast. The porcupine's return made the *Sacramento Bee* and *The Union*, not to mention both county papers, *The Messenger* and *The Booster*. Two-inch headlines, with photos of the animal on its hind legs begging, wearing fake Christmas reindeer antlers. The game warden got his picture in the papers too and played along, saying he'd relocated the animal thirty miles away.

My family never even mentioned the accident. It was like it didn't count against me. That turn in the state road had been the scene of two accidents that year alone. The boys weren't local; the funerals were held in another town. When Moonstar brought me home from the hospital we passed the place where the car went off the road into the river. There were heaps of flowers, and balloons tethered to a tree. I was edging out of the cab of the truck when both Sun and Little came running out of the house. There had been a phone call that Sun had answered. A voice said, "You know where your porcupine is? Try the road going to the dump."

I slid back into the cab and Little and Sun got in too. When we got close we could tell where P and P was by the ravens. He'd been run over, not once but again and again until most of his quills were broken and his body flat like a lump of string. Little had to scrape him into a cardboard box with a square nosed shovel. Then we drove down a dirt road until it ran out and we buried the porcupine there. Little took a photo of the gravesite hidden among a clump of ferns.

Moonstar announced we were going up to the cabin for Thanksgiving. "Would you like that, Roscoe?" I didn't care where I went. I could move my arm; the cast was off.

Moonstar's district superintendent gave us a ride up to the snow line. He was going up to cut his Christmas tree, he said. I was always surprised at how differently we as a family were treated, now that Moonstar was a teacher. Small convenient kindnesses were an everyday thing. I'm going down below; can I pick anything up for you in town? Can I give you a lift? We didn't hitch anymore, or apply for food stamps, either. We had a truck, credit cards and a checkbook. We hadn't seen a hippie for months, where we lived now. Had they stopped coming up to the mountain? Not likely, I thought. They were waiting for summer.

There wasn't a lot of snow yet at the end of the paved road, but enough to ski on. I was lagging behind. Little had the supplies on the sled. Moonstar and Sun skied ahead, racing each other. I couldn't keep up. My right side was hurting. I couldn't let go, quit thinking about the photos Little took of me when I was huffing and sniffing. And I had my share of thoughts on why I did what I did. "Poor self image leads to substance abuse." Sun had said that five times now. "He's easily led," Moonstar said. Little didn't comment at first. He'd enlarged the photos. You could make out the ring the gas can opening had made, pressed against the skin on my face. My lips were chapped raw, skin scaly, my nose peeling like I had a sunburn. It didn't do any good to tear up the eight-by-twelve photos; he'd just print more. Pin them up in my room. Dumber than dumb, I heard him say to Sun. He was right. Once, after huffing, someone suggested a circle jerk. I copied what everyone else knew how to do, but I went flat. It was no use, though I went on pretending, making the motions. I wondered if this was something else I wasn't going to be able to do, like my reading too slow, that I'd never catch on to. Maybe Moonstar was right; maybe all that gas and glue did burn up my brain. Those other boys that died, I wasn't even sad; I never thought about them. Dumber than dumb.

I reached the cabin last, past dark. I didn't think I was going to make the last mile. Maybe I didn't want to. I felt sick for the first time in days and finally vomited up my guts, but it didn't make me feel any better. I still had to see my father.

He'd hung the old construction lantern with the green glass at the door to guide me in. I took my time. Let the story be told and retold so I wouldn't have to hear it again myself. I hadn't got the old feeling back that I'd come home again to our ridge. 6,040 feet. The place where I belonged. I didn't believe that anymore.

Sebastian met me at the door, gave me a clap on the back, and then, for the first time, half a shoulder hug. "Roscoe," he said, louder than he meant to, making us both jump. We shook hands. The others watched us.

There was nowhere else to go in the mountains: you had to face yourself. I split wood, but my timing was off: I'd miss the round, or worse, get the ax stuck. I made an eight foot snowman and skied the slope like old times. Moonstar roasted Cornish game hens for Thanksgiving dinner and made a pumpkin pie in the wood stove. I didn't have an appetite. Thursday. Friday. Saturday. I'd been working it out in my head. The accident was like the beginning of something, not the end. It wasn't just that I was lucky I didn't die; I had to change. Where can I go from here, I kept thinking. How do you change? There was nothing for it but to try and find out.

Sunday morning we got up early to get ready to ski back down. I didn't feel any better, but I didn't feel any worse. I knew something was up when Moonstar got me alone. I was stacking wood in the shed. "You're staying with your father, Roscoe." If she expected any argument, I wasn't giving her one.

When they left, Moonstar went first, then Little with the sled. Sun slowed where the trail curved, and waved back to me with her ski pole one last time before she disappeared into the trees.

THE JAUNT

My father and I started slow, like we'd never met before. He didn't bring up why Moonstar had dumped me up here on the ridge with him: that she'd got a job teaching fifth grade in Cold Springs and I was embarrassing her. The hippie era was over, she'd been saying lately. Not for my father.

There were no storms yet so we worked outside in the clearing about fifty yards from the cabin, where he'd felled two dead sugar pines for next year's wood. We spent the daylight hours limbing the trees, then bucking the logs up into rounds and rolling them closer to the cabin to split up. I'd never understood before how silent he was. He didn't speak. I was coming to realize it was my mother who did most of the talking for him: "Roscoe, Sebastian wants you to go down to the river and check the dredge," or "Sebastian says the roof needs shoveling off." I was the oldest, I was almost as tall as he was, and I'd never minded having to do the work that went with living in the mountains. Neither had my brother Little or my sister Sunflower; it was only Moonstar who had a problem with the Sierras, that there wasn't another living soul within sixteen miles of us.

We took hourly breaks, sitting on a round, looking back to the cabin. A foot of snow covered the flat part of our clearing. Under the trees, where the trunks held the heat from the sun, the ground was bare and dry, just pine needles and broken grass. The dead winter sun came out unexpectedly and then disappeared in the grayness of the clouds. Not a leaf left on the apple trees: they'd been pruned already so they wouldn't break from an overload of snow. Sebastian smoked his calabash pipe: it was always in his mouth when he worked or when we were on the move.

Once we quit and went inside the cold dark cabin, I'd start a fire and he'd light a lamp. The cabin was fourteen feet by twenty-four, with a loft where Little and Sun and I slept. The cast iron stove looked too big for the main room. A curtain on one side closed off the bedroom; the double bed almost filled the space. A door led into the lean-to where the flush toilet was. The place was small but it was easy to warm. We didn't keep the stove going unless we were inside and could use up the heat.

Everything had its place. After we took off our leather boots we'd hang up our coats and sweatshirts behind the stove, put the gloves and wool hats on the drying rack. I'd fill the wood box for the night and make sure there was kindling to start the fire in the morning. I'd sweep out the place through the front door into the snow. He cooked supper. That surprised me; Moonstar had always done the cooking up here. I liked what he cooked: the first night was pasta with olive oil, garlic and anchovies, and I was surprised again when he said after supper, "I ate that once in a two star restaurant in Italy. Michelin rated." He saw I was waiting for more and went on, "Roscoe and me. We were celebrating making staff sergeant." Roscoe was his Army friend I was named for, and I knew Sebastian had spent two and a half years in Europe between his tours in Southeast Asia. He did the dishes, too, using the teakettle of hot water from the stove to rinse everything good.

Supper was the only meal he ate. For the others I was on my own. Breakfast was coffee, three or four bowls of the puffed wheat we packed up in twenty pound bags, and Sebastian's specialty, drop biscuits. He'd make eight or nine dozen at a time, one pan after another. Flour, shortening, baking powder and salt, powdered milk. He never measured anything, mixed it all up in a big five quart yellow bowl. I'd spoon honey over the biscuits and eat them until I was full. Lunch was my favorite of favorites, Spam.

The first big storm hit on February eleventh, two days before I'd turn thirteen. I'd been back since the long weekend of Thanksgiving. The wind was howling, making the cabin shake like it was going to take off like a kite, but I felt comfortable for the first time. At 6,040 feet elevation, locked into a wall of snow, I was safe now. I didn't have to remember the past, nothing about the entire year of 1981. No dumb moves huffing glue and sniffing gas. It wasn't me drinking beer in the '71 Mustang that went off the road and rolled and killed the other three kids. I was going to start over. None of those things happened up here. Maybe to the Roscoe McAdams who'd been living down in Cold Springs at 3,000 feet, but not up here.

We were sitting at the table. My father had the parts of the carburetor of our chainsaw spread out before him on a clean rag and was reassembling them. I was musing, my mother called it that when I stared into space, and my eyes focused on the *National Geographic* photo hanging on the wall. I couldn't see much with just the one kerosene lamp lit, but I knew it by heart, could click it into focus like I was watching a slide show. Moonstar standing in the foreground holding me: I'd been born three weeks before. The center pole of the yurt with a lantern hanging from a nail. My father in the background shadow.

I didn't remember living in the yurt, but I remembered my father building the cabin a couple years later. My brother Little was born at the UC hospital in San Francisco two years after the photo, my sister Sun in Miner's Hospital, Nevada City a year after that, when my mother was visiting someone there. I could understand why she'd changed her name from Annette to Moonstar now, if it truly worked that you really could erase the first twenty years of your life that way.

The earliest and clearest I could remember was a day my mother left the front door open a crack to cool off the place because it had got too hot in the cabin; with the wood stove, it could get to 90 degrees sometimes. I had been out in the shed with Sebastian and had come back in but was still dressed in my outside clothes. Little was already talking then, so I must have been four. I wandered outside again. I didn't know where I was going. It was snowing, the wind was blowing enough to sail the big flakes sideways, like flapping moths.

I knew I was outside the clearing and past our ski slope, probably on my way to the river. The old snow was hard, so I wasn't sinking in much but leaving enough of a trail to follow back. My father had taken me on plenty of jaunts before. At one point I got confused and climbed a young fir tree to see where I was, like Sebastian did. Get a better view. That's when my father caught up. He climbed up into the tree too. "Where are we headed?"

"Just taking a jaunt."

"This is going to be a blizzard, a whiteout, I like being outside when this happens too. It's different every time." The tree was swaying in the wind so we held on, watching the flakes flutter around us. "The snow is our friend," he said.

When we got back to the cabin, Moonstar had her town dress on and was stuffing clothes in her pack. "I've had enough. I'm leaving with the kids as soon as this storm is over. This was a bad idea, a bad choice, Sebastian. This is worse than prison. You found Roscoe this time, but what about next time?"

I could tell my father tried to be sociable. He'd comment on things. "The thermometer fell to 19 last night." He'd take his pipe out of his mouth to speak. "Good for the snow pack." But some mornings it was like Sebastian had forgot I was there. I'd eat breakfast. Quietly put more wood in the stove. I could hear him turn over by the squeaks of the mattress, hear the pages turn when he was reading. He'd read anything—old textbooks, histories, paperbacks, anything. We had hundreds of books we'd accumulated over the years; we collected them like we were getting our winter wood in. He liked to read lying down in his bed, by the hour; no, by the half day. I knew he was awake by the smoke from his pipe. The flush of the toilet. I read, did my lessons. We had got back on the old footing; I was calling him Sebastian. I'd never asked what he preferred: Moonstar always wanted Moonstar. At noon I'd start making noises, banging a lid on the stove, scraping my chair. Then he was up, his bare feet hitting the floor as hard as a gust of wind against the cabin's wall.

I never gave it a thought now, filling the chainsaw with gas, that a couple months ago I'd been putting my nose in the same kind of can, knocking myself crazy. Huffing glue with a plastic bag over my face. But sometimes I saw things when I was reading. It was like I had two books in my lap, the one with words, the other that went through my head like a set of photos that always began with a red ladybug, small as a period.

I woke up: my father was shaking me awake by the shoulder. "Roscoe. Roscoe." He hadn't lit a lamp but I could see him from the light around the lids on the stove: Sebastian in his long johns and the stocking cap he wore to bed. The open loft was the warmest part of the cabin. "You're having a nightmare."

"I'm awake, I'm awake." I knew where I was now.

He sat down on the bed. "You were yelling. Do you remember what you were dreaming about?" I shook my head and said no.

"I always could. In mine, I was falling from a high place, and it didn't stop until the end when I hit the ground. It took me months, years to get through most parts of that dream, because you get another variation of the first nightmare when you use one part up. You have to go through the whole thing again." It was the longest he'd talked since Thanksgiving. He must have sat there another ten minutes without speaking.

I had another nightmare the next night. He banged the broom handle on the ladder rung to wake me up. But this time I remembered what I was seeing when I slept. It was the ladybug, bigger now, flying in the open window of that Mustang back in October.

The night after that I slept some but woke up very early. I went down the ladder and scooped out the ashes in the stove. Filled the bucket, being very quiet. I didn't remember where he'd got the stove, but there was a story. It was old, had a patent date, 1898, under the Bridge and Beech, St. Louis on the top of the ash box. Six lids, a huge oven and three warming shelves in back. Did he wheelbarrow it here after he drove as close as he could get with the truck? I put my boots on and carried the bucket of ashes out. There was a frozen crust on the snow and I went as far as the first row of apple trees. Red coals still glowed in the ashes, and I spread them in two big X's and one O along the first row of trees, put the bucket on the chopping block, and started walking north to pass the time. It was too dark and it was still snowing, huge flakes, big as pancakes, as Sunflower would have said. Snow covers the landmarks but you can still tell where you are by how long it takes you to get there, so I was about three miles—sixty minutes, twenty minutes a mile—from the cabin, still on the spine of the ridge, going higher up, the trees thinning a little where the sugar pines stopped and the spruce started. Still under 7,000 feet.

Sebastian was in the shed when I got back. He'd lit a lamp, which was unusual: he liked to wait to see if the sun would appear so he wouldn't waste kerosene. I sat down on the chopping block, stomping my boots against the floor. There was no neater work bench: every tool had its place and that's where it was. He was screwing on the fins to a windmill. For years he'd tried different ways to get electricity to the cabin, but so far the only way we'd ever got the forty watt bulb to light up inside was with a generator. That kept the area around the cabin in a thick fog of diesel fumes and the thump thump of the motor drove everyone crazy, Moonstar especially. "It would be nice to have light, but not at the expense of our health and sanity. We don't have to live up here, Sebastian. You like the primitive too much. If it wasn't for me we'd still be living in the yurt."

I got so I was afraid to shut my eyes at night. Up until now, I'd never been able to remember what had happened during the accident, and I was sure I didn't want to find out in my dreams. But every time I let my eyes close I was sitting in the back seat of the '71 Mustang, moving down Highway 49 too fast, the back rap of the exhaust pipes throbbing. I'd read slow, the way I liked, keep my lantern on all night; that helped.

And I did chin-ups. There was a section of three quarter inch galvanized water pipe bolted over the door that we used for chin-ups; it had been part of the plumbing from our spring to the kitchen sink. I'd pull myself up until my arms and elbows made a good 90 degrees. Again and again. Push-ups, too, interspersed with sit-ups, tucking my toes under the wood box. Sometimes Sebastian would stop reading and watch me from his bed. "You're not putting your chin over the bar. Quit trying to climb the air; keep your legs straight down." Once he got up from his bed and did a couple to show me. "It's all in letting your head notify your body that you're going to need some extra power." Sometimes I'd come in the cabin and he'd be doing chin-ups. "You caught me," he said once. He could do them perfect, by the dozens.

At supper, frittata with canned spinach, his favorite vegetable, Sebastian said he could hear the storm dying, though the wind was beating against the walls harder than before, driving the wood smoke back down the stovepipe and into the cabin. It got so smoky we had to open the front door. You couldn't see anything outside: it was like someone had hung a flannel sheet over the door, the white was so thick. It was hard to know if it was still snowing because the wind didn't allow the snowflakes to land before throwing them back in the air.

"I was thinking," Sebastian said later on. "We need a good outside task. Tomorrow we could snowshoe to the Studebaker, get it running. It's been three weeks to the day." It was good news; it was better than that. I got my leather boots out, and the MJB can we kept the bear grease in. Took a dab with the tips of my fingers and started rubbing it in. Rubber insulated boots made your feet sweat too much; we never bought them. The grease smelled bad, so I moved my stool in front of the open door. I started on my father's boots. We only killed animals we could eat, so we'd have to be as hard up as the Donner party to shoot a bear. The meat was awful, rank, grained with green yellow fat. We must have got this bear grease in trade, probably from Mr. Elliott.

He'd shoot one if it was going after his porch freezer, and then render the fat down. I greased the leather bindings on our snowshoes too. My father didn't use skis in new fallen snow. It was too much like work, he'd say. I set out the clothes and equipment we'd need to get to the Studebaker.

Whenever my father would say we had an interesting task ahead I'd stop whatever I was doing to listen. I don't know why he always said *task* for certain things we had to do. Tasks were different. Cutting winter wood, that was just something that had to be done, like breathing, just part of living up here on the ridge; it didn't fit under task or chore or work, even, but we'd get up in the dark for a task. "Dress accordingly;" he'd use those exact words, too. Winter was always layers of clothing and a rain poncho if we were going to get wet. And always a couple of pairs of wool socks that we rotated when our feet got wet, fastening the damp socks with safety pins to our long johns. The trick was to avoid sweating and getting overheated. We always carried snowshoes, no matter how cold or how thick the crust was. Twenty-below sleeping bags and a pack with water and food. Skis were fine in the open, in daylight, without a storm.

On the ridge, a thousand feet could make a big difference. In our part of the Sierras you could get three feet of snow at six thousand and only six inches at forty-seven hundred. That's where my father hid his '53 three-quarter ton Studebaker pickup, low enough so he could get the truck out after an early spring thaw, even sooner if it hadn't been a wet year.

We moved through the forest fast, as if we were being chased. On a task we took the most direct route, right through the trees, straight up or down the ridges, faster and faster, until we'd end running.

I was keeping up okay; I'd been worried about that. I liked the tasks, but I liked the jaunts better. On a jaunt we planned our route, getting out the maps, spending hours working out the most interesting way to get somewhere. Just for fun, my father showing me the mountains.

Sebastian could follow a compass like other people could tell time with their watches. Storms, wind: weather didn't stop us. In fact, the wilder the blizzard, the better. We'd follow creeks, old logging roads, even animal trails to find some place. "Here it is," he'd call out, and point out what was left of an old flume, or some headstone sticking up out of the snow. "They took a million dollars out of that part of the creek." Or, "Six million from that shaft over there." He talked a lot more on a jaunt.

I took biscuits and cans of Spam. He could go all day with just a mouthful of water. I needed something to eat, even if we were just going out to take a look at the river. A jaunt could turn into anything. Five days, sometimes. A task was a task: we'd finish and go back to the cabin.

The '53 Studebaker was hidden in a nest of brush by an old logging road. You could be within five feet and not see the pickup. There was a canvas tarp over the cab and a slant roof over that that sloped the snow off into a ravine. There were no walls, just the four unpeeled logs holding up the rusted corrugated tin roof. This was as close to the cabin as we could get it. My father had got the truck the year I was born, in 1969. He'd paid a case of Lucky Larger beer and a carton of Pall Malls to Mr. Elliott, who was his friend and the caretaker at the Upper Seven Aces mine. We had a new ninety-six month six volt battery, so we never had trouble starting the old truck up. All we had to do was remember to come here every few weeks. One crank and the flathead six would turn over, ready to roll. Sweeter than sweet. Never on the fritz. My father talked like that sometimes. I think he was imitating Mr. Elliott, who always said things like that. We'd check all the fluids later.

It was kind of odd, sitting in the cab in the middle of the forest, snow as far as you could see, with no possibility of going anywhere. It was sort of a letdown, once we got there after a five and a half mile trot. I mentioned that to him, and he just laughed. "If you think this is boring, pretend it's summer, Roscoe, and we're driving the shortcut down to the river." We both laughed at that. By August the dirt roads in the back country were almost undriveable, two feet of dust that would rise up to the sky like a thick fog, filling the cab with so much grit you couldn't see where you were going. Just to breathe you had to wet a farmer handkerchief and tie it over your nose and mouth. And go slow, slow, in the lowest gear, like feeling your way in the dark, trying not to get high centered or rip a slice in your oil pan on a sharp edge of rock. It took all the early weather in September and October to even start to settle the dust and turn it into mud. Then, with a cold snap the end of November, the ground would freeze and the dust would lie dormant until the next June. I preferred the winter.

We decided to sleep there, me in the cab and Sebastian in the bed of the truck. He could sleep anywhere. If we stayed over and didn't go back to the cabin, it meant a jaunt. Maybe.

Sebastian was already out of his sleeping bag and sitting on the bumper of the truck when I raised up from the front seat. I watched him carefully shake his morning instant coffee out of a plastic pill container into the palm of his hand. From where I was, it looked like a chaw of tobacco. With a quick motion he threw it to the back of his open mouth, chewed twice, and then took a long swig of water from the canteen. "Damn good cup of coffee," he said, knowing I was watching.

I put my boots on and went over and washed my face with a scoop of snow. Opened a can of Spam, slid the rectangle of meat out onto the gray metal hood of the truck, whacked off a hunk and put it between two halves of yesterday's biscuit. With a drink of tea from my canteen it was more than a good breakfast.

I had stopped asking Sebastian if he wanted some, because he never did. He had a USFS map spread out on the other side of the hood, tracing something with his finger, saying the names of places he covered with his thumb. He showed me the route, moving his bitten-down fingernail along an old trail I'd never been on. Follow the ridge to the symbol of a pick and shovel—that was the Yellowjacket Mine—and then past Wolf Creek to the Despair. Then straight down toward the middle fork of the Yuba, stopping at the Upper Seven Aces Mine for a visit to Mr. Elliott. About a nine hour jaunt from the Studebaker. It was gloomy out, overcast, like the world had only two colors, gray and white.

We left fast, carrying our snowshoes, using the early morning cold to run on the frozen crust of snow. My legs were almost as long as his, but I had to push to keep up. But he'd stop ten minutes on the hour for a rest up, just like he was still in the Army. I usually spent the time bent over, my hands locked on my knees, trying to catch my breath. He'd relight his pipe and lift my wool cap off so I'd cool off quicker.

We took longer at the Despair, looked around. At the mine portal you could see the steel rails disappear into the tunnel. Bottle diggers had found the old mine dump, and a few mounds of rusty cans showed through the snow. I kicked the cans loose and looked for broken off bottle necks. I just picked up the blue ones first, my favorites, milk of magnesia bottles, Vicks. Then dark green from champagne bottles. I found a long piece of copper wire and strung the bottle necks on it until I had a couple of dozen.

There were parts of rusted water tanks sticking out of the white snow, and worn out equipment from the stamp mill, like there had been a lot of activity here once. When the Despair was running, there'd been a hundred nineteen miners working three shifts here, Sebastian said.

A half mile up was what was left of the town. It was hard to believe that from the 1870s to 1890s there'd been 6,500 people living here because of the Despair. Schools. Stores. Churches. Houses. Gone. The only traces now were a few foundation stones, a cemetery, old growth stumps, and like always, the kind of broken down apple trees that lived forever. It made you think.

We took off again, moving slower, going zigzag up the side of the ridge. We made it to the top before the yellow sun popped out of the gloom like a bird, turning the gray sky blue. The best part about winter was you could move over the snow fast as the crow flies and not see the mess people had made of the forest: the clearcut sections, old growth trees mowed down so all you could see now were rows of replanted pine all the same size, like a big tree farm. Logging roads that wandered everywhere like fresh scars in the red dirt. Burns. Logged-off places where they'd harvested pines and firs and left slash for acres and acres. The very worst scars were left a hundred years ago by the hydraulic mining companies, whole mountainsides washed away to nothing for the gold, until hydraulicking was finally made illegal. It took ten feet of snow to hide those mistakes.

The crust turned to slush with the sun, and we had to put on our snowshoes and sunglasses. I asked if we could stop at the Christmas tree, and he nodded. We had to go out of our way but it was worth it. I spotted the tree at a couple hundred yards. Black oak, maybe my age, fifteen or twenty feet high. Strands of glass bottle necks hanging from the leafless branches dazzled the eye; it did look like a Christmas tree. I'd put buckets of broken colored glass around the trunk, too, but they were still covered by snow. "I'll be a minute," I said and took off, liking the way the tree came into focus as I got closer. Bottle necks. PG&E insulators. A branch was starting to grow around a pair of horseshoes I'd hung on it years ago, when I was six or seven; Sebastian had stood me up on his shoulders. I walked around the tree a couple of times, enjoying myself. When I noticed a bare limb I swung the wire a good whorl over my head and sent the bottle-necks up into the branches. They flew like those clusters of flashing blue dragonflies you see in the summer over still water.

Going downhill is harder than going up on snowshoes. Your shins ache, then throb so much you think some bone is going to snap off. You had to be careful everywhere in the snow — drop offs, rotten snags, holes, pits, avalanches — but I knew my father would be on the lookout, so I daydreamed most of the two thousand foot drop in elevation to the Upper Seven Aces.

I tried to stay away from thinking of Moonstar. I'd start feeling bad whenever I did; I didn't know why. I wasn't thinking so much about Little and Sun anymore. Maybe my brain cells had been burned up by the gasoline, like they said. I never ever thought about the other three boys in the '71 Mustang. Sometimes I'd think of girls, not the naked ones in the magazines, but the ones I'd sat near at school, the mole on the neck of one of them, the pitch of a giggle.

I tried to think of something else, what food would Mr. Elliott have for us when we got to the mine, but it didn't work. Moonstar appeared. First thing she said was about Sebastian: "Doesn't he have to grow up like the rest of us?" There was no getting her out of my head until she had her say. "Mama's boy" — she called him that when she was yelling at him. But she didn't get mad when I asked her once about his friend Roscoe, what he was like. She had met Roscoe and Sebastian the summer after she graduated from college. She paused, which was unusual; she had an instant answer for everything. Finally she said, "Ask Sebastian."

When I started smelling wood smoke, I opened my book of facts on Mr. Elliott to get ready for our visit, check if I was up to date. He was born in the Sierras, but in the southern part, near Yosemite National Park. His father's blacksmith shop had been where the Ahwahnee Hotel was now. My mother said the Yosemite Valley was a tourist trap, but our grandparents had taken us to Yosemite once, so I knew the exact place where the blacksmith shop had been. Mr. Elliott could remember the Valley Indians, old women that still ground acorns in the big rock mortars along the Merced River so they could make acorn mush when they didn't have the money for flour.

It was impossible to keep Mr. Elliott's stories in order: he bounced around back and forth from his time in the US Navy Submarine Service during World War Two forty years ago to last week when his dog Soupbone got skunked. There was no question you could ask to lead Mr. Elliott back to where he started. You just had to keep track of all the parts and put the whole story together later. Even when I had the facts in order, I was still never sure of the questions to ask. Sebastian was no help; he'd just nod sometimes, or laugh.

Mr. Elliott had come to the northern Sierras in 1928, the summer before his last year in high school, to work in the mine his uncle leased, the Brass Knuckle. That was the first time he laid eyes on these Northern ridges. And he never left for the next fifty years except for his time in the Navy. Mr. Elliott could be funny. He'd known Sebastian from the time my father was sixteen and working summers for the Forest Service, knew his complete story, which was more than I knew. Mr. Elliot's first name was Lincoln, and Sebastian called him Linc.

We got there at the Upper Seven when it was almost pitch black, but light was coming from three windows: there'd been power lines going to the big mines up here since 1909, Sebastian had told me. When I asked him why, when we didn't have a line to our own cabin, he said because the mines had paid big money to the power company: with electricity they could produce more gold.

I hoped we were still in time for supper. I was ready as I'd ever be for the talk. I always tried to be watchful, keep a distance from the story so I could remember better what was said. I knew it wasn't my place to give an opinion. My questions should be aimed at keeping the conversation going or asking for more information on some part of the story. You allowed the talk to find its own way. My father said some famous person had called this kind of conversation the language of men: the idea was to trade experiences or stories, real or imagined, back and forth in order to fill in all the important blanks about themselves until they were caught up to the present. Sebastian thought it was their funny stories that told the most about a man, and stories about women the least. My mother didn't know about this. She called it pointless, especially when Grandfather talked, which was pretty nearly all the time when the family was together. "Why is it men have to keep defining themselves over and over?"

Mr. Elliott was glad to see my father. Shook his hand twice, stamping his right boot on the wooden floor while he did. When he noticed me he pulled me out from behind Sebastian and took me under the single bulb hanging from the ceiling.

"You grew another foot," he yelled, waking up Soupbone, asleep under the table. "If I knew you were coming I'd of baked a cake." That made me laugh. Because he would have baked a cake, and he and I would have shared it between us, but there had been no way to let him know we were coming. I started to relax some after we took off our coats. My father lit up his pipe and I scratched Soupbone's ears. Mr. Elliot was shoving frozen dinners into the oven of his wood stove. He talked as he moved around the room making highballs for himself and my father and opening a bottle of what he called sarsaparilla, which was orange soda. He liked to use the old words when he had the chance.

Mr. Elliot was shorter than me now. Welterweight, when he talked about his short boxing career in the Navy. He probably still weighed one forty-seven, three pounds less than I did. He was bald with a white horseshoe of hair, his nose was mashed at the bridge and he didn't have that many teeth left. He wore old faded clothes, but he always smelled clean.

I stood out of the way. The room was filled with furniture crowded so close you couldn't sit down on anything, rocking chairs locked together with the settee, and end tables so loaded down that every flat surface had stacks of newspapers and old envelopes. He got his mail a couple of times in the winter from the PG&E lineman, when he checked for breaks. Mr. Elliott started moving things off the round oak table until he got down to the green and white checkered oil cloth. Then, selecting fresh second pages of *The Messenger*, he spread them over the table. He liked the section where the sheriff's office listed all the calls for the week and he'd read out loud when there was a lull in the conversation. "Here's one. 'Missing husband found in Calpine. Reports he was drugged and kidnapped.'" We all laughed. Then he replaced all the condiments. The accident had been in the paper. Mr. Elliott knew about it. He'd given me a look like he knew.

When we could smell the gravy burning on the meat he took the aluminum trays out of the oven and slid them onto the table. He kept his kitchen and front room past warm; both my father and I were down to our undershirts. I noticed my upper arms were bigger than my father's now. His were like sticks of muscle; mine had biceps. The part that looked in the right proportion to the rest of him was his head, the big red beard and the pile of dreadlocks that my mother said looked like an osprey's nest.

Our dinner trays were red hot but Mr. Elliott and I dug in, blowing on our forkfuls before we carefully snapped off bites of meat to keep our tongues from getting burnt too bad. No one spoke; there was just the sound of forks scraping against the aluminum trays or the two of us grabbing slices of bread out of the plastic wrapper. I finished my first and started on my second tray. My father was only half done; he had to press himself to finish one of these Hungry Man sized dinners. Mr. Elliott was sopping up the gravy and applesauce on his with a piece of bread. He got up to check his barometer. "Dropped two more points," he said. He'd tell if a storm was coming by that instrument. My father and I were wind forecasters, southwest wind and if the sky was covered with nimbostratus clouds, along with how far the temperature had dropped below freezing.

I slowed down, not to finish before my father. Started spearing the green beans one at a time. Spooned the mashed potatoes leisurely into my mouth. Eating for Sebastian was like work he could never finish. I looked the other way when he passed some of his roast beef to the dog. When I put down my fork I gave a loud sigh of satisfaction. Sweat was rolling down both our foreheads.

"It's dessert time," Mr. Elliott announced. "Can I interest anyone in a chocolate cream pie?" We all started laughing, and I raised my hand like I was in a classroom. He went out to the back porch to the freezer and came back with two eight inch pies and set one in front of me. My father didn't eat sweets; he didn't have a single cavity. I had cavities.

Mr. Elliott was getting ready to talk. He rolled himself a cigarette. A lot of the tobacco fell out of the paper before he could get it licked together. He never noticed. My father lit his pipe. Mr. Elliott warmed up, skidding off mining to take up the county assessor, who'd sent him a potholder with his name stenciled across both sides, which he held up for us. "I'm going to vote for that son of a bitch," he said, and he slapped the potholder onto the table. "It's the only free thing I've ever got from this goddamned county." I didn't even notice I'd been scraping my aluminum pie pan clean until Mr. Elliott pushed his half eaten pie over to me. I glanced at the clock on the wall. We'd been there almost three hours already and it felt like just ten minutes had passed. I was getting sleepy from the food but I had to stay alert. I got up and put another chunk of pine in the stove. Went and took a leak and sat down to take my boots off; my feet were too hot. Gathered up all the trays and pie pans and scraped them off into the dog's dish and then gave them a scrubbing. Mr. Elliott saved everything, egg cartons to string.

They were waiting for me to come back to the table for Mr. Elliott to start. I always knew where he'd left off the last time we were here, but he never did. I didn't have a good memory for schoolwork or even what day it was but I knew exactly where someone had left off on their tale. "Now where was I?" he said for the second time. He liked that I could tell him.

"Mr. Elliott, the bank crash had occurred in 1929 and you were in college in Stockton at that Methodist school. Because your father had died you had to quit school to help support your mother and two younger sisters. You went back up to the mountains where you'd worked that summer before and got a job at another mine that was hiring. It was your first night in town and you had an attic room with two other men at Mrs. Swann's boarding house and you were eighteen and one-half years old."

My father nodded and Mr. Elliott said, "That's right." He relit his cigarette, the tobacco flashing up like a grass fire, sending sparks onto his wool shirt and burning small brown holes in the newspaper covering the table. "I was laying on my bunk up in the attic with the door open to the balcony to catch the night breeze. I could hear the music from the bar further down the street. People were walking by, their words floating up. Three cars passed; someone honked a horn. Chips Flat was a town then with population of 2,500 people and a thousand of that number were single men working in the mines and looking for a good time. There were about a hundred women who came up to provide the entertainment on paydays. Remember, this was 1930, the start of the Depression, hard times were upon us. I was lucky to get a job as a mucker on a ten-hour shift, six days a week." He stopped and scratched the dog's ears.

"It was a warm September, a Sunday night. I would go on the graveyard shift at twelve. There were others beside me in the boarding house. I could hear them moving around their rooms, someone was running a bath.

"I'd already visited Chips Flat back in the summer I worked for my uncle because the women were supposed to be prettier up there . Got drunk as a skunk a couple of times. Engaged in fisticuffs there twice, both of which came to a draw, I thought. Flirted with the girls, but I knew enough to keep my fly buttoned." He thought a minute. "You'll remember I got the clap when I was sixteen from a whore in Sonora." He left a space for me, so I put in, "Betsy, twenty years old, and it cost you three dollars."

"She later married a surgeon," he went on. "They used to make movies in Sonora, westerns;

Gary Cooper was in one. It brought people from all over, just to watch and because you might get picked to be an extra. Hollywood people liked Sonora for western movies because of all the old buildings." He stopped to collect himself. "Where was I?"

"First night at Mrs. Swann's boarding house in Chip's Flat," I put in.

"I was lying there when I heard the screaming. I listened as it got closer and louder. I don't mean regular screaming, but full out, like it had a echo, loudest I ever heard. I'd learned a long time ago not to take notice of trouble that didn't concern you, but I couldn't help myself, I had to see what all the commotion was about, so I went out on the balcony. The boarding house was on the end of Main Street within about a hundred fifty feet of the nearest bar.

"There must have been ten or twelve women moving down the street toward me screeching, and then I noticed a girl out in front, staggering toward the boarding house. She was trying to scream too. There was a crowd of townspeople following behind all the women. When the woman in front, a girl, I could see now, reached the steps she collapsed, and all the other women fell silent.

"The girl, Lucille, I found out later she was only seventeen, was going with a miner named Smitty that was on the first shift at the Sunrise. I have not used the words whore or prostitute here, you'll remember, and I rarely mention the word love. But Lucille did that night. 'I love him. I love you, Smitty.' She tried to yell her I love yous as she crawled up the stairs. I was standing right over her two stories up, and I could see blood trickling out her nose and mouth.

"Someone was running through the crowd, and it was the mine doctor who had given me the physical to get the job. Just as he reached the girl she gave a great cough and spewed out a mouthful of blood all over the doctor. He cursed and took out his handkerchief and wiped his face. One of the women yelled out, 'She's swallowed a bottle of lye.' The doctor yelled back, 'Well, don't just stand there, call the sheriff; he's the county coroner, too.' That was my first night in the town of Chips Flat."

I waited. Mr. Elliott was still going over his ending in his head, so I asked, "Is lye a poison?"

"You bet it is. My mother used lye made out of stove ashes to make laundry soap, but this was store bought. It's a corrosive; it would eat up your insides if you drank it. We never had a funeral in town for the girl. Her folks came up and took her body away; I think they were from Oroville, over in Butte County. Smitty was fired from the mine, blackballed from the whole district by the end of the week. The mine owners professed to follow Christian principles. Smitty had had his way with her, and that was what happened in those cases. The last I saw of him he was packing his duffle bag and saying 'What did I do? I hardly knew her.' I had seen him around town when I came up from my shift. He was a lady's man. Slicked his hair with perfumed pomade and wore pressed clothes. Sweet talker."

We all thought about that for a while until I said, "Mr. Elliott, it's almost twelve o'clock." We had never owned a TV; Moonstar wouldn't allow it.

"Damned if it isn't; it's time for Benny Hill." This was a funny program that came from England every night. I never understood a lot of what was said, but you didn't have to understand to laugh. Benny Hill was always chasing after girls. There was a sidekick, an old bald short man that Benny was always slapping on the top of his head. Sometimes there were no words, and everyone was chasing each other double time. It only lasted a half hour, but our sides would hurt from laughing, mine and Mr. Elliott's.

When we were visiting Mr. Elliott, Sebastian and I would shovel off the catwalks for him. Nail loose boards back on. There were probably fifteen buildings still standing on the site and twice that number already fallen down; "In disrepair," Mr. Elliott said. At least three acres of rusted metal roofs. Bunkhouse. Cookhouse. Office. Blacksmith. Sheds and stables and garages. Old mines like this were bought and sold every ten years or so by doctors and dentists who used the places as tax write-offs but never reopened the shafts.

In the buildings that still had stoves, Sebastian and I made fires to get the snow off the roofs. Sawed up the limbs that had come down off the pines from the wind. No chainsaw, so we used a two-man saw, a Swedish banjo as Mr. Elliott said. It was good working with my father; I could daydream away on the other end of the eight-foot saw sliding back and forth like the tick tock on a grandfather clock. We stopped for breaks and water just like we were on the trail. "Don't eat snow, Roscoe; go get a drink from inside." The back and forth of the saw would have put me to sleep if it wasn't almost dinnertime. Mr. Elliott was whistling inside, baking bread and cakes and pies. For lunch we had Hungry Man turkey dinners and I had two pieces of chocolate cake and a wedge of apricot pie. I could barely move, but we went back to work to finish our sawing and then put up a new TV antenna on the crown of a white fir. My father went up the 100 foot tree limb by limb to attach the thing. He didn't like me climbing too high; he said I didn't pay attention enough.

We had a supper to remember, smoked ham steaks, sweet potatoes and enough baked bread to fill me up. He and my father had five highballs instead of the usual three. Mr. Elliott talked but didn't stay on the subject. He started in World War Two, the time during a patrol when the captain surfaced the sub and the crew went topside to get some sunshine. With most of the men relaxing naked on the deck, a Japanese plane came out of the sun and dropped a bomb on the sub. Mr. Elliott took a long drink and then started in on a different story about when he dredged with my father on the Yuba River. The gravel paid off and they went halves on a seventeen-ounce nugget.

He went on with that story, one I'd heard before, until I interrupted, which was something I didn't like to do. "Mr. Elliott, what happened when the Jap plane dropped the bomb?"

He looked like he didn't recognize me or remember the story. After a minute, he said, "It didn't explode; it bounced off the conning tower: bent the rail all to hell, and we got out of there, dove and stayed under for another four days. We weren't even safe in the middle of the Pacific Ocean."

We didn't visit Mr. Elliott during the summer. He usually had a woman living with him once the road was open. My mother knew of Mr. Elliott as a friend of my father's, someone he'd worked with in the mines as a young man, just from the rare times Sebastian ever spoke about him. Never met him. But she knew of him also as that nutcase who'd come into town for a wingding that left everyone talking. He was a legend. He'd drive into a place in his open Jeep—you could hear him for miles once he got on the blacktop because he left his snow chains on all year long—and the racket from the loose chains hitting against the steel body hard enough to make sparks was like a signal for every barfly in the area to watch close for what bar he'd go into. Drinks were on Mr. Elliott.

Two summers ago when we were staying in Blue Canyon we'd watched Mr. Elliott pass by, clanking, honking his horn, folks cheering from the sidewalk. My mother shook her head. "Pathetic." I stepped into a shadow. They kept the bar open late when Mr. Elliott was in town. Let him rest up on the billiard table. I used to watch him carrying on sometimes from the back window of the bar but made sure he couldn't see me. The very life of the party, Moonstar would have said. Wannabe hippies, a few ashram members and the freeloaders in attendance. No one went thirsty when he was around. He'd sleep it off in one of the shacks in town, and when he'd wear out his welcome after a few days he'd go back to the Upper Seven Aces. I tried to keep an eye on him, but I had no intention of ever going up and shaking his hand and saying hello. Up on the ridge was one thing and down in town was another. One time I was passing by an old battered trailer and heard a noise. I looked in the open door and there was Mr. Elliott, naked on the bed with a naked woman on either side, all asleep or passed out. I couldn't help looking, and then he opened his eyes. He knew who I was. Later that day I saw him pass in the Jeep: with the noise, I'd had plenty of time to hide. There was girl with him, young, with a shaved head.

It took three days for Mr. Elliott to get to his best stories, about highgrading. I was patient, didn't ask any questions. Lifting some family rock: at the Sunrise that meant stealing goldbearing ore from the mine. The miners who worked underground had to strip off their street clothes, put them in their lockers, and walk naked through the manager's office to the changing room where their diggers were and their rubber boots, helmet and carbide lamp—those were the clothes a miner worked in. Then they'd take the skip, something like an elevator, down with the rest of the shift to the level they were working at. "The twenty-three hundred foot level, say, where we were following a seam that looked promising. We'd drill. Set the charges and blast, and then muck out the rock into an ore car, and then do it all over again. For ten hours. The drilling wasn't water-cooled then, so there was a lot of quartz dust, which coated your lungs with glass. So from the dust, most of the miners got silicosis. Later there were a lot of lawsuits over it, but no one ever beat the owners or the state of California. Got a question?"

I knew enough not to interrupt; I shook my head no.

"Coming up to the surface, we stripped off our diggers and took a shower; it was tradition that the company supplied the bars of soap. Then naked we walked through the manager's office, where the shift boss or one of the engineers, any company man, was stationed to watch: they knew all the miners' tricks. 'How's the wife?' they'd ask, or other questions about our families to see if we could answer around a mouthful of highgrade. Look us over careful under the glaring light to see if we had any ore hid in our armpits or between our toes. One mucker wore a leather truss. That's like a jock strap but more substantial, a leather belt to hold in your bulging rupture. I've seen those bigger than a softball, hanging out of someone's lower stomach. That truss was noticed right off, and the mucker was told to take the thing off, which he did. He wasn't hiding anything, but you can bet the next time he was."

Mr. Elliott gave me a wink. "Well, how did the miner get the highgrade out, you're wondering? If you didn't already have an arrangement with the superintendent or foreman for a split, one way was to fill a glass vial, that's like a test tube but smaller, and stick it up your ass. Gold was at thirty-five dollars an ounce since 1932, and we were making something like forty-five cents an hour. Hell, even in 1962 me and your father were making only a dollar and a quarter an hour. You had to steal to live then, to feed your family. Everyone stole. I take that back; I know one person who didn't, out of the hundreds of men I worked with over the years."

I knew to ask my question then; we'd done this before. "Who was it?"

"He's sitting right here in this room." We took a breather and Mr. Elliott went on to a different story.

That night Benny Hill played a doctor in a hospital. All the doctors and nurses are taking each other's clothes off and chasing each other around when the little bald man comes into the emergency with stomach pains. After swatting the little man on the head for a while, Benny Hill decides to operate. Mr. Elliott and I were rolling on the floor at this part: Benny is using a toilet plunger and a bike pump and a carpenter's saw to perform the operation. Then, when the patient finally recovers and pays his bill, Benny follows him out of the hospital onto the sidewalk. Not speaking a word, he shows the patient his bare wrist and points to the patient's chest. Pantomimes he's lost his watch and it's inside the patient. The old man takes off his own watch and hands it over to Benny and runs off down the street. We were laughing so hard tears came. My father didn't crack a smile. He could have been in the next room.

After Benny Hill I fell asleep, but I woke up later and they were talking. I heard my name, Roscoe, but it wasn't me, it was my father's friend they were discussing. I knew my father had spent some of his leave up here in the mountains with Mr. Elliott before he went back to the war the second time, and that Roscoe had come up for a visit. Mr. Elliott had met Roscoe before I was born. I listened awhile to the words but couldn't put them together into an idea. My father said something I couldn't hear. Then I fell asleep.

Snowshoeing back to the cabin, I had a chance to think things over, dot the i's and cross the t's in the stories. The snow was soft and we sunk in a foot with each step; my father was breaking trail. It was hard going uphill, and I'd eaten too much breakfast. Six fried eggs, potatoes, I don't know how many strips of bacon or how much toast. I thought I was going to spit up, but I kept my mind off the way the food was rising up into my throat. I knew when I ate it I was showing off: when Mr. Elliott would ask, "More?"

I'd nod, yes. It was a game I was going to lose. My father had just watched. He'd told me more than once, "You're like me; you have to learn everything the hard way, by your mistakes." I hoped that wasn't true. I'd already made too many.

We were halfway to the cabin when the storm hit. One minute there was no wind; then suddenly the trees around us were bending double, throwing the snow off their branches into the air. I heard limbs snapping off; the snow was sharp, hitting me in the face like glass. I'd never seen it like this before. We kept going against the wind and I kept close to my father; it made me worry, not being able to see anything. Sebastian stopped, waited up for me, yelled in my ear, "We're going to have to hole up." He just stood there the longest time. I knew he had his compass out; we were never lost. Never. These were our mountains. He started moving again, slow, through the forest, and I followed.

The trees were acting like they weren't rooted to the ground anymore, doubling over, moving around, changing places with each other. I knew what Sebastian was looking for: a tree with branches low to the snow, with a good-sized cavity formed around the trunk, where we could wait out the storm. We'd done this before.

We were in a clearing, only a few trees around us now. I put my back to the wind and cinched up my hood to protect my face. When I looked again, I couldn't see my father. The snow was so soft I was sinking past my knees. I slipped my snowshoes off and crawled under the branches of the nearest tree. There was a good space, but Sebastian wasn't there. Under the branches, out of the storm, it was like the wind had stopped blowing. I backed out and crawled to the next tree. There wasn't much of a space under that one. He wouldn't leave me out here alone; I knew that. I yelled his name, knowing it was no use against the wind. He wasn't playing hide and seek; storms were serious. The only other tree was an old dead cedar snag, no shelter there. I put my snowshoes back on and started making circles around the trees, keeping my eyes on the shape of the surface. I kicked against a bump and it was Sebastian, the tip of his snowshoes. He was already covered with snow, and I dug him out. I brushed off his face with my hands. His eyes were closed like he was asleep. I felt the artery in his neck and there was a beat. I couldn't figure out what was wrong until I got my arm under his shoulders to sit him up. There was red on the snow under his head and on the big cedar limb underneath that must have snapped off from the snag. There was a mass of thick blood oozing down into his dreadlocks. I shook him. "Come on, Dad. We've got to get moving. Come on, now."

I took his snowshoes off and dragged him over to the cedar with the cavity. Slid him down the five foot slope to the base of the tree. We were out of the wind, but it was too dark to see. I tried to light my candle but it wouldn't stay lit. Patience, he'd say. I put him in his sleeping bag first, then wrapped his head in a towel. Patience and calmness. Then got in my bag, but kept hold of his wrist to feel his pulse. Relax. I couldn't leave him in this storm, go for help; I'd never find this place again.

I don't know how long I slept, but the storm was still raging outside when I woke up. I was still holding Sebastian's wrist. The pulse was beating hard against the inside of his arm. I wasn't worried. He'd come awake and we'd be on our way. Then all of a sudden I remembered. All of it. Squealing around the curves in the Mustang, the three in the front seat, the middle one reaching back to me with the quart of beer so I could take a swig, the speck of red that flew in through the window. When the kid who was driving reached for the ladybug and caught it in his cupped hands and the car left the blacktop and sailed out over the bank, we were all hooting and laughing. I hadn't been worried then; I knew no one could die.

SEBASTIAN'S SON

It took two days and a night to move my father through the storm to the nearest blacktopped road. I took off my snowshoes so I could slide him down the ten-foot berm left by the snowplow and then I waited on the road for some vehicle to pass. I'd got Sebastian into his sleeping bag right after he was hurt, and once it got light the next morning I'd started dragging him along on a fir branch I used as a travois. The storm was still raging like it was never going to let go of the mountains, never stop piling up new snow; it had dropped close to three feet so far. I waited, hunkered down, taking off my glove once in a while to feel the beat of my father's pulse against his warm neck, brushing the snow off both of us. He had taught me how to remain calm, calm in these situations.

A Dodge pickup appeared out of the blowing snow, and it stopped for us. We rode in the bed, the chains making that slack catching-up sound between the treads and the ice on the road. The driver's wife and three little kids kept looking through the back window to see if we were okay. I had left our packs and gear. Behind the cab, out of the wind, I didn't feel the cold any more. It snowed all the way down, from 5000 feet at the road to the 2600 in Nevada City. The driver went right to the old hospital.

They knew what to do at the emergency room entrance. Three nurses pushed open the double door with the end of the gurney. We scraped the crusted snow off the sleeping bag and slid him onto the gurney and lifted him out. The pickup driver didn't know me but he gave me enough quarters to use the phone. I thanked him several times and he left. I was still standing there in the emergency room when the wife came back in and handed me two one-dollar bills and hurried back out. I didn't find out their name.

They wheeled Sebastian into a room and unzipped the sleeping bag and peeled it down off his long body. His big nose was sticking up out of his red beard; the coils of his dreadlocks were hanging off the edge of the table. The doctor came in then and examined the wound on the top of my father's head, still oozing blood that showed on the white paper covering the table. When they started cutting his hair I stopped watching and went off to find the phone.

We were not to call my mother when she was at school, but I did anyway. When she came on the line, I didn't give her a chance to say anything. "Sebastian is hurt bad; we're at Miner's Hospital. Moonstar?"

"I heard you; I'll be down."

I phoned my grandparents next. I was lucky; Grandmother answered. Grandfather didn't like me. Whenever he answered he'd say, "Hold on. Hilda, it's for you." I tried to be gentle with her, she was the kindest person I'd ever met, but there was no easy way to tell her about her son. She said they'd leave right then and drive up from Sunnyvale. I went back and saw they were cutting through the laces on Sebastian's boots with a scalpel. A nurse came out and told me they were phoning a specialist.

I spent one of the dollars for a candy bar in a machine and ate it down without even tasting the sweet. Then felt sick and sat down in the waiting room and that's all I remember until Moonstar was shaking me awake. "Roscoe, go wash yourself." I ignored that and told her about us snowshoeing through the storm and how the wind had dropped a branch from a cedar snag down on Sebastian's head. She was wearing her school clothes, the blue pants suit and the white shirt with a tie. Her blond hair was cut so the ends rested on her shoulders. Red, red lipstick, the color of blood. She'd stopped wearing the floor length dresses, the single long braid down her back that reached her hips, silver rings on her toes. Queen of the hippies, then. "Go wash your face, Roscoe."

I did what she said. In the lavatory I had to scrape the black pitch from the fir branch off my skin with my fingernails; the soap didn't work on tree sap. I washed and then washed again. In the mirror my mountain clothes looked faded out and raggedy, but they'd still kept me warm enough: long johns, two tee shirts, wool sweater and jacket. Trousers with the knees gone, wool socks, leather boots. Wool is the best in a cold country.

I went back out to the waiting room. Moonstar was reading a magazine. I was suddenly pissed off at her, as if the accident were all her fault. We ignored each other. I slumped in a chair, noting my mother's perfect posture, and fell asleep again.

I woke up with a start from the yelling. It was Moonstar and Grandfather; a nurse with a clipboard was watching. "I can't believe you didn't put him on your medical insurance." Grandfather's face was red.

"We weren't legally married; we were never married, Elmer, that's why."

"Why do you go by McAdams, then?"

"It was just easier."

"Sweet Jesus, after all this time? All right, then I'll pay for this," Grandfather said to the nurse. Grandmother saw that I was awake and came over and gave me a kiss on the cheek and then a hug. Then she got between Grandfather and Moonstar like a referee. A doctor came in then and gave his okay on something. Elmer went off to make phone calls. When he came back, Sebastian was going to a veterans' hospital, close to where my grandparents lived.

I stood up then. "I'm going too," I said. Before my mother could open her mouth to say no you're not, I shouted, "I'm going." My mother turned around and walked out.

I went in the ambulance with Sebastian. Once we got on Highway 80 at Auburn and I watched out the back window as cars passed us on the freeway, time speeded up; the traffic moved fast; you never saw the same car twice. My grandparents tried to stay behind us: I could see their faces through the windshield of their DeSoto sometimes. The attendant kept touching knobs, making little adjustments to the monitors that were attached to my father by wires and tubes.

When we got to the Veterans Hospital there was another problem. Staff Sergeant Sebastian McAdams had been AWOL from the US Army for the last fourteen years. Declared a deserter. I was too beat to want to think about what that meant. Grandfather spent more time on the phone, then had a meeting with someone else. Sebastian was admitted that night. They said he was in a coma.

I was getting a second wind. When we stopped to eat, I ate most of the extra large pepperoni pizza. I didn't try to make any conversation, they both seemed so tired out. When we got to their house, it looked the same as always, clean, a lot of space, no knickknacks. I was to sleep in Sebastian's old room. Grandmother gave me a pair of Elmer's pajamas to wear. I was taller now at thirteen than he was. I showered and brushed my teeth. There were a lot of framed photos on the walls. Some were Little's.

Grandfather had taken up photography years ago and had got my brother interested too. Just thinking of Little made me feel better. When I wanted to annoy him I'd call him the smartest kid in the school district. At eleven, he probably was. But Sun would point out that she hadn't taken the test yet to prove she was the smartest.

Later, when I got back to Cold Springs from Sunnyvale, I'd forget and start thinking my father was still up on the ridge in our cabin. That I could hike over for a visit. That he wasn't in the Veterans Hospital, still unconscious. I wasn't pretending those times; it was real. Sometimes I couldn't stand my thoughts and my eyes would fill up and I wouldn't even know it. It could happen anywhere, but more often when we were all together. When we were eating supper, sometimes Moonstar, Little and Sun would pretend they didn't see the tears running down my face, dripping off my chin. It wasn't until I couldn't help making noises because I couldn't breathe that Moonstar would say, "You're excused, Roscoe," and I'd leave the table. At school I'd walk out of the classroom and go home.

Once Moonstar came into my bedroom after what she called an episode, while I was lying on my bed staring up at the ceiling. "I want you to see someone, Roscoe. You can't go on like this." I'd decided not to speak when she brought this subject up again. Someone was a shrink. We'd already had our shouting match after I came back from Palo Alto. Another when I took off for a couple of days once and walked back to our cabin on the ridge. When she turned and left the bedroom I knew neither of us was going to take this any further.

The wonderful thing about daydreams is you can most times work out a happy ending. Not always. It's risky to be too happy. Endings are always hard to get right; they have to fit the situation. With nighttime dreams, nightmares, you're stuck with what appears when you fall asleep. The latest thing to happen inside my head was that nightmares had taken over my daydreams. It was like an alligator had opened its mouth and those jaws lined with pointed teeth had closed around my head; there was no escaping. That's when I cried and couldn't breathe right.

Clever Moonstar did trick me into seeing a psychologist. I was shooting baskets with Little at the school, waiting for Sun to finish orchestra practice, when up came our Ms. McAdams with a guy who didn't look like a teacher, long grey hair in a ponytail, glasses, and the mountain uniform of flannel shirt, jeans, boots. I'd made myself stop thinking that any man she was with was screwing her. "This is Arnie," Moonstar said. "Arnie, my oldest son, Roscoe." It's too hard to be rude, so I shook hands, and so did Little. I understood Moonstar was nervous because she started explaining why we called Little Little, how Grandfather wanted us to call him Big Elmer to tell them apart, so we used Little Elmer for my brother. Then we dropped Little Elmer to just Little. That was the brief version: my mother could go on for ten minutes, so I took aim and tossed the ball at the hoop, and my mother stopped talking. Arnie caught the rebound off the backboard and we started playing Around the World. Moonstar wandered off. Arnie was worse than I was with a basketball. Little was already getting high school coaches to come and watch him, even in sixth grade. Big as I was getting, I didn't play sports.

So for a half hour we shot baskets. Arnie got Little talking this and that. I wasn't paying attention: for the first time, I was winning. Sinking twenty footers like I was born to it. But I didn't notice the fucking tears were streaming down my face until they started splattering against my fingers. I was so used to it I just wiped my face with my sleeve and took my shot. Arnie stopped talking and watched me sniveling and asked, "Are you all right, Roscoe?" It pissed me off, the question, and I yelled, "No, goddamn it, I'm not all right." "Why aren't you all right?" he said back. I was caught up with the words, not their meaning. "Because my father is sick." I couldn't use the word coma. "That's not your fault, Roscoe." I had to pause a minute. Think. I never thought it was my fault. We were caught in the mountains in the worst storm anyone could remember. A fucking limb from a cedar snag came down and brained my father. Sebastian always rejected talk about luck, chance, fate, destiny. There was no such thing, he claimed. You have to ignore all that or you end up with just another religion. Accept what you can't change. Then get on with it. But Sebastian was lying in the Veterans Hospital in Palo Alto. I wasn't going to accept that, never.

I was calm now. I held out my hands for Little to throw me the ball. It was my turn. "Cool," I said. "I'm cool."

"Why are you so angry, Roscoe? So hostile?" Something snapped in my head like the fan belt on a car engine, that exact sound, and I wanted to kill the fucker. I must have gone for him, because all at once Little had me down on my back, and I was trying to break the hold he had on me. But I was too crazy and couldn't work it out. You have to think and think again when you do battle, or you're just dumb muscle. All the years we'd practiced hand to hand with Sebastian, and I'd broken the first rule: think. "I'm cool now," I told Little. "Let me go; let me up."

Arnie leaned over us. "I can help you, Roscoe. Here's my card." He handed it down, tried to set it on my stomach. I could read the card, Dr. Arnold Lund, Psychologist, and I went for his hand, snapped my

teeth at his fingers. Little held me down some more
until I could get control.

One Wednesday after school I didn't go home;
I just kept walking, through town, past the house
and down the road. Took the shortcut, straight up
the ridge, headed for our cabin. When it got dark,
I just sat down, my back against a tree. I must have
slept, but I didn't dream. I woke up at first light and
continued the climb all the way to the cabin. But once
I got there I couldn't go in. I just sat on the chopping
block by the front door. I thought I should call on
Mr. Elliott, but that would just make us both too sad,
seeing each other again so soon. It had been only a
couple of weeks ago that we'd driven his old Jeep
down the hill and then got the bus to Palo Alto to
visit Sebastian. I had thought if anyone could bring
him back, Mr. Elliott could. I'd told Sun I was going
so she and Little wouldn't worry.

We'd made a pair, the two of us, going to the
VA hospital. We'd both tried to look our best. He'd
cleaned up, shaved, and he wore his double-breasted
jacket from the gray pinstripe suit he'd bought in
1946 when he was discharged from the Navy over
his newest bib overalls. I'd found a wool overcoat at
an estate sale, camel hair with a label from England,
that fit my five feet ten perfect now. There were a
few rich people in these mountains, but they kept
separate. They retired here, bought five acres below
the snow line and built big houses, got bored, then
sold or came up just in the summer.

I should have known better. You can't keep
repeating yourself. When I had gone down the
first time, when Sebastian was admitted into the
Veterans Hospital, I'd stayed with my grandparents
in Sunnyvale. I'd thought my father would wake
up, and I wanted to be there. It didn't happen that
way. Not for a minute. After almost a week, my

grandfather told me I'd have to go to school down there, not just spend my days at the hospital. I was sleeping then in Sebastian's old bedroom, from when he was my age, and there was still a lot of stuff of his in the dresser drawers and in boxes in the closet. It made me feel better, having his things so near, until the night I was looking through some photos taken during the two and half years he spent in Europe when he was in the Army.

He didn't tell many stories about that time, but there was one about climbing to the top of every damned tower and dome in Italy: he and his buddy Roscoe, going up a thousand marble steps, the Leaning Tower of Pisa, another tower in Bologna, the dome of St. Peter's in Rome, the turret on some palace in Urbino, I don't know how many more. I was looking at the photos from then, enlarged to nine-by-twelves; Grandfather must have done that. Sebastian standing next to a big statue of a man on a horse. At a table at an outdoor restaurant. With a pretty woman, both smiling. He looked so different then, Army haircut, clean shaven. I'd only known him with his full beard and dreadlocks. Some photos were labeled on the back: Vicenza; Rimini; ski resort, Switzerland. Then a close-up of him and his friend, just their faces. On the back, Roscoe and me, Munich, 1967. I looked a long time at that photo. Sebastian. Roscoe. I looked at it and at myself in the mirror on the dresser, the three of us. My dark hair, cleft chin. I didn't just look like Roscoe; I was Roscoe.

Then was a knock on the door and Grandmother came in. She saw the photo I was holding and she looked with me at my reflection in the mirror. She knew. I could tell by her face. She must have always known. I should say something. Anything. Is Roscoe my father? But I didn't. Everyone knew but me. I left the next morning for the mountains.

*　　*　　*

I'd thought it would be different with Mr. Elliott, but we ended up just standing there at the foot of the bed. "Dad, look what the wind blew in, just guess." I tried a lot of openings like that. It was hard on Mr. Elliott, being in the room: there were three other veterans his age laid out in the other beds, in comas too. He tried. Told his best stories for a hour. His third wife, who got religion and left him for a 38-inch midget preacher. The time the two of them almost drowned in the Yuba River, swept downstream, lost their five inch dredge. "You'd be proud of your boy, Sebastian, dragging you all the way from the Lucky Dog to the Henness Pass road."

I heard him say that and I thought, but did I save a dead man that would never come awake again? I couldn't stand thinking that. He'd been here for almost two months now, and the VA was going to put him in a long-term facility. They couldn't do anything more; they'd operated twice now.

I remembered how the next morning after Sebastian was hurt I didn't know what to do next. I couldn't leave him to get help and ever hope to find this place again in a whiteout. I pretended I was him and did what Sebastian McAdams would do, broke off a big fir limb and lashed him in his sleeping bag to it good and started dragging him down the ridge. When I couldn't go any further, I sheltered us under a tree and rested. It didn't matter, night or day, during the storm; it was all one. I pretended we were talking as I pulled him behind me "You remember that time when we were dredging on the Middle Fork and I was wearing my new wet suit? A September afternoon, we'd been working a gravel bar since morning with nothing to show for it but heartache, as Mr. Elliott would say. You were sitting on a creek boulder smoking your pipe and I was standing in the water waiting for you to say, 'Let's call it quits,' when what do I see in the rocks right next to your boot but a piece of white quartz the size of a tennis ball loaded with high grade. It had come down river a long way and was rounded and oblong. And I said 'Hey, Boss, Supreme Mining Engineer, you're almost sitting on more money than we made all week and you're too lazy to reach down and pick that nugget up?' We both had a big laugh over that." And then, as I was dragging the travois across a frozen creek, Sebastian said something back. Just a couple sentences.

I dropped to my knees and waited, listening, my ear close to his face, but there weren't any more words. I felt a lot stronger then. Using the compass, I took the shortcut to the road. I didn't want to hurry and make a mistake. I understood if I got hurt we were both finished.

I listened to Mr. Elliott end his story. Sebastian didn't look like himself anymore. Beard shaved off, dreadlocks gone, face as white as the sheet, even thinner than he was before. Hooked up to all the machines. Was this even my father any more, laid out in the hospital bed? There were no mountains for cover here. He was out in the open now.

Three men in white coats came hurrying into the room, talking like we weren't there. Mr. Elliott and I stepped aside when they got close to Sebastian's bed. "This is exactly what I'm talking about. Head trauma. Motorcycle, probably." The doctor had a clip board and a stethoscope around his neck. "Should have been gone from here a week ago. We can't do anything for him, and we need the bed. No helmet, most likely. Too smart for that; we get cases like this all the time. It's ridiculous." He looked at the paper on his clipboard. "In fact, this guy is the VA at its best, a classic. Absent without leave from the Army the past fifteen years, and here he is: we had to admit him."

Mr. Elliott spoke up. "This man has every right to be here." Because he was hard of hearing, he was talking too loud. "He did two deployments in Vietnam. Two years fighting in that bullshit war in southeast Asia." The doctor tried to say something but Mr. Elliott went on. "Were you ever in the service, you sorry son of a bitch? That boy won the Silver Star and I don't know how many Purple Hearts. The only thing you ever got from the government is a fat paycheck." The three men backed out. I could see Mr. Elliott was shaking, he was so pissed off.

I could hear someone coming down the hall fast. A woman came through the door and her high heels clattered to a stop. She was looking us over. I don't know what she was expecting, two troublemakers probably. We were docile but stood our ground. "May I help you?" she asked.

"We're just visiting my father, Ma'am."

"Sebastian McAdams," Mr. Elliott added.

The woman surprised me by putting out her hand. "Irene Chester. My office is down the hall."

I put out my hand too. "Roscoe McAdams."

"I'm Linc, Lincoln Elliott, hardrock miner and king of the northern mother lode." He went on with his spiel; Mr. Elliott always said too much and tried to be too funny with someone new.

I interrupted. "Ma'am, what's going to happen to my father?"

"We don't know. Your father could come awake anytime, or he could remain like this. If you want the truth . . ." I nodded. She looked right at me. "It's possible he could die without regaining consciousness."

There was nothing to say after that. We all just stood there. "Why don't we go down and have a cup of coffee at the nurse's station?" Ms. Chester said. I went over to say goodbye to Sebastian. I had the feeling it was for the last time. And I meant to pat him on the hand, but I bent down and kissed him on the forehead. I surprised myself; I didn't remember doing that before.

When Mr. Elliott and I took our leave from Ms. Chester, she held onto my elbow. I had mentioned, when I was able to wedge some words into Linc's tale, that during the storm Sebastian had spoken to me. She asked me now what he'd said. I knew the words, but my eyes started gathering water like they were pouring sweat. I didn't want her to see me like that, so I turned toward the window. "He said, 'Hot damn, Roscoe, this is going to be a jaunt to remember. Take ten.' A jaunt was a surprise hike with a destination, and take ten was the break we took every hour." They already knew that, but I said it anyway.

We had to change buses in Sacramento, and there was a four hour wait. We got there about seven in the evening. The March sun was almost down but the temperature was a steady warm 66 degrees. I'd taken off my wool overcoat. My school clothes still looked clean and ironed.

I knew I had to stay alert, keep an eye on Mr. Elliott, who was getting tired out. If he was born in 1911 and this was 1982, he was 71: not old, but he needed to sit. A lot of places around the bus station were closed, but we found a Chinese restaurant and went inside. I couldn't interest him in supper, but he ordered a beer and then another. Before I could finish eating my cashew chicken he'd downed five beers. I noticed it didn't take a lot of alcohol for some people to get drunk, and Mr. Elliott was one of them. I got us headed back to the bus station to wait. There were a lot of people milling around outside, a lot of commotion, cars passing slow, yelling, folks just standing around in the almost dark.

The first thing Mr. Elliott does, he goes up to a girl who doesn't look much older than me. He's having a high old time, both laughing. Mr. Elliott waves me over. "Roscoe, I want you to meet Cinderella." Like a fool I put out my hand out and she takes it and puts it inside her dress between her warm soft breasts. It's the funniest thing Mr. Elliott has ever seen, and he starts hooting. I try not to be embarrassed. But I am. I don't pull away my hand; it's like I can't let go. "The meter is running," Cinderella yells, and I drop my hand. Then I'm really embarrassed. I can still feel the beating of her heart in my fingers.

Mr. Elliot takes me aside. "Roscoe, for Christ sake stop calling me Mr. Elliott; you make me sound like I'm your grandpa or something."

"Okay," I say. All I want to do is get home, back to the mountains, get on the bus and go to Nevada City where we parked the Jeep and drive on up. Linc goes off down the street where he thinks there's a drug store. I can hear the women talking. It's a slow night. When a car slides by one of them says "Show time," and they all start marching up and down the sidewalk, making their short skirts bounce so you can see their underclothes. I try not to look.

Linc comes back waving two pint bottles and yelling, "Meet my best friend, John Barleycorn." The women take swigs from the bottlenecks sticking out of the brown paper bags. It's almost a hour before the bus leaves, but I'm almost giving up hope that I can get Linc on it when some big guy appears out of the building next door and grabs the first bottle and smashes it on the sidewalk and then the other bottle. Silence. From everyone but Linc, who puts up his fists, "Come on, you son of a bitch, that was my liquor." I know Linc the former welterweight is exactly 147 pounds and the guy who Cinderella calls George has to weigh twice that and is fifty years younger and ten inches taller, all information that might not matter if you were sober and knew how to defend yourself. George is watching, his arms to his sides, as Linc is dancing around in front of him, already panting for breath.

I've seen these kind of situations play out before in town, so I know if someone intervenes the situation is always made worse. But I can't leave Linc. And I can't let George hurt him. George doesn't want to be anyone's entertainment: he's noticing cars are stopping and people are coming out of the bus station to watch. One of the women says something to George, who turns away, and Linc hits him with a combination of five punches that land hard against George's face. It's like Linc's fists are bugs splattering against a windshield, for all the damage they do. George reaches out with his left hand so fast I don't see the movement and grabs Linc by the neck and lifts him up off his feet. Without planning anything, I step in close and use my elbow on George, hit him sharp in the solar plexus, and it takes him by surprise and knocks the wind right out of him. Then there are sirens, lights and police and I grab Linc and we run into the bus station. "I had him," Linc says as we found our bus and got in it and sat down. "Pimps can't fight." I keep my thoughts to myself. I'm thinking of Cinderella.

Heading northeast out of Sacramento on the bus, I thought how the forty-niners took this same route a hundred and fifty years ago, dreaming of gold in those mountains ahead. Gold fever. Even now, people still bought the myth that you could get rich mining. I knew better; I had spent hours freezing my ass off in the Middle Fork with our dredge, looking for gold. But I'd seen it happen in Cold Springs.

When Moonstar moved us down there, but before she started teaching, most of the mines around town, mines that had produced hundreds of millions of dollars since 1857, had been abandoned. Then all of a sudden gold went up to a thousand dollars an ounce, and it was like April Fools Day kept repeating itself every twenty-four hours. Some old writer from the gold rush days said that a mine promoter is a liar who owns a hole in the ground. This time it was the smartest people in the world, engineers from the electronic plants in Santa Clara County, who decided they'd go to Cold Springs and consolidate some hardrock mining claims and walk right into the tunnels and fill up their empty sacks with high grade. They were going to need about a hundred miners to start out with, to timber and pump the old shafts clear of water. They opened accounts at the store and made down payments on old shacks and set crews to fixing them up for the influx of new people. All at once, the shining new pickups in town outnumbered the old beat up mountain wrecks.

Folks poured into not just that town but every other town nearby to find work. The bars were full and they had to buy new desks for the schools. The Consolidated Mining Corporation held an open house at the company building by the portal, kegs of beer and all the hot dogs you could eat. You can bet that Little and Sun and I were there. People in Cadillacs and Mercedes drove up and went into the office. Through the window I could see new stock-holders signing checks and getting those beautiful stock certificates, like they'd just graduated into the millionaires club.

A thousand dollars an ounce. I hiked over to the ridge to see Sebastian and keep him up with current events. The last time he'd cashed in, he was getting six hundred dollars an ounce for the gold he dredged out of the Yuba River, more if it was a good size nugget that a jeweler would buy. I knew he was holding back about ten ounces of flour gold, thinking the price might go even higher.

The two of us went down to see Mr. Elliott at the Upper Seven Aces Mine. My father let me do the talking and I gave the words all the flourishes and whirls they deserved. Linc just listened, sipping his highball like he hadn't heard. "There's a fool born every minute and two thieves to fleece him," he said finally. He jumped up and went into his bedroom and came back with a pint jar, the bottom reinforced with duct tape, half full of dust. "Roscoe, you take this into town and sell it for me." He tossed the jar in my lap. "And you sell your dust, Sebastian. That company will go bust; you can take my word to the bank. The world price will drop back. It's a commodity: you can't earn interest on gold coins in a drawer like you can on savings in a bank. Those fools are absolutely right that there's a hundred million dollars worth of ore in those mine shafts, but it'll take five hundred million to turn it into gold ingots. "

My father trusted Mr. Elliott's judgment, and we hurried back to the cabin. Sebastian gave me his jar of dust and I shot down the ridge as fast as I could go, record time of three hours and nineteen minutes. I was to take both jars to a friend of Mr. Elliott's, Johnny Bock, and he'd handle the transaction. When Johnny saw the jars of dust he grabbed his fedora and we drove to the most popular bar in the county, always full of folks, locals and tourists, on a Saturday afternoon. Johnny was another of those old guys who time and events had passed up, or used up, Sebastian didn't know which, an old hardrock gold miner who'd mined in Utah for uranium too, a B29 nose gunner over Japan in the war. Sebastian said the thirties Depression and then four years of war had left folks sort of stunned, especially if they'd stayed in the mountains. It was not a place to think you could watch the world go by and take it easy.

When I carried the expensive glass-cased scales into the bar, Johnny didn't have to make any announcement of gold for sale. He set the scales up on top of the pool table and started weighing out the dust by the pennyweight. The talk died suddenly, and people watched. You could almost hear the grains of gold pour into the brass plate with little tings, twenty penny-weight to the ounce. "I'm selling by the pennyweight for sixty dollars. By the ounce, Yuba River gold for eleven hundred dollars, cash. An investment you'll never regret." I wasn't sure what was going to happen next, but folks started lining up. The next thing I knew I was running to the store for more envelopes to put the dust in. Johnny made a nice profit. So did my father and Mr. Elliott.

In nineteen weeks the boom burst, just like a pine tree splits into a thousand pieces when it's hit by lightning. Consolidated Mining went bust when the price of gold dropped so much they couldn't pay the electrical bills for pumping out the shafts, and the investors and stockholders saw their dreams bottom out at one and half cents a share. Even I felt bad, though I hadn't had any money to invest, and Cold Springs became the saddest community in the county. The mining hoax hadn't fooled my mother. She'd always said the Gold Rush proved that the only people making money from gold mining are the people selling the shovels.

With Moonstar, out of sight was out of mind where Sebastian was concerned. She wouldn't let Little go down for a visit, wouldn't allow the subject to be brought up. Her reason was she didn't trust Grandfather. "Remember last time? How Elmer kept Little after his appendicitis operation for seventeen months?" And when Sun tried to ask, all Moonstar said was, "It's a waste of time. Your father is comatose; ask Roscoe."

I promised Sun I'd take her down the next time I went. But I had no intention of going back to Palo Alto in the foreseeable future. It was just too hard. And I couldn't stand thinking about finding that photo with Roscoe and my father. Grandmother had found out from Mrs. Chester that I'd been down to see Sebastian and hadn't even bothered to phone her. She wrote me a letter about her disappointment. She ended saying she was still visiting Sebastian every day and that Irene said to say hello.

June came. I didn't pass; I was going to stay in the eighth grade another year. I'd missed too much school, they said. I didn't care any more. Moonstar had been transferred to Ophir Flat Elementary and we were going to move there in July. No one there would know I'd been held back. I dredged the summer with Linc and we found a nugget wrapped around a chunk of quartz as big as bar of soap. He said I was a lucky partner.

After Labor Day I felt like a bear having to wake up after hibernation. School was going to start, and I had to get our cabin on the ridge ready for winter. Finish splitting and stacking the winter wood in case Sebastian was able to come back. I could tell myself that; I could tell myself anything and believe it. I got the dredge out of the river and stacked the wood in the shed.

And Sun gave me my annual pep talk. She ended up like always, yelling, "Roscoe, you behave yourself." I knew she was right, so I'd listened. I had to be careful. I'd fucked up before. Then the accident with the Mustang. That's when Moonstar took me out of school, sent me up to stay with Sebastian in the cabin last winter. Doing something stupid again wasn't going to bring back Sebastian. I was going to be fourteen next February; this had to be my last year in elementary school. So I took an interest in the books they gave me in class. I knew it wasn't going to be easy for me. Nothing was. And I stopped comparing myself to Little and Sun, and that helped. I didn't smartmouth back whenever a teacher asked in amazement, "You're related to Little McAdams?"

I was treating school like an unhappy task where you have just to put your head down and get the job done, and mostly that's what I did. I understood that Sebastian, my unarmed self-defense instructor, was a deserter from the Army, that Moonstar was no longer the woman in the *National Geographic* photo, that I wasn't my father's son. That my father could be dead soon. I understood, but sometimes it was too much for me. One time I started feeling worse than bad and set about getting some supplies together, thinking I'd better take a jaunt. I left a note for Sun, walked out of the house one morning and made it to the Upper Seven Aces before dark. Linc didn't know I was coming, but I'd brought us a feast: a dozen big red onions, some cans of anchovies, a couple loaves of Italian bread, and a twelve pack of Miller High Life in those clear bottles Linc called tall blondes. All the things he liked best. "Christ almighty, you hauling freight now?" he said when he saw the load on my packboard.

He picked up one of those red onions, wiped it on his sleeve and took a bite like it was an apple. I didn't drink as many beers as Linc did, but I had my share. I told him the latest on my father, who had started to move his legs some. I noticed the conversation was lagging; he wasn't keeping his end up. It just wasn't the same without Sebastian there. He'd never said much, but he made a difference somehow. I suppose Linc missed him too: I'd heard him call Sebastian *son* sometimes. As far as I knew, Linc didn't have any children: he just married women with kids. At midnight we watched Linc's half hour program from England, but Benny Hill didn't make us laugh very much. Chasing after the young women didn't seem very funny any more for either of us.

"Did we have dessert?" Linc asked. "How about a frappe?" I'd been thinking of something else and didn't hear at first. He left and went out to the back porch where his freezer was and came back with two ice cube trays of his ice cream. He was famous for his vanilla ice cream; he made it in an old wooden hand-cranked machine. He said it tasted better if you had to sweat a little for it. We squirted chocolate syrup on top and dug in. I always got headaches when I ate ice cream too fast, but that didn't even slow me down. We ate in silence and when we finished neither of us said anything for a long time, until I asked, "Linc, did you know I wasn't Sebastian's son?" He heard me but didn't answer. I didn't think I could ask the question again. He lit up a readymade cigarette out of the carton of Pall Malls I'd brought.

He looked at me and then he looked at his hand holding the cigarette for a while. "When you get older, you'll understand better. People can get in the most god-awful fixes, the kind that are impossible to understand for anyone watching or even for the folks that are in the situation. You have to imagine your own self doing the same dumb thing. That's the trick to it. Understanding you can do worse, and probably will. There are a lot of small steps people take leading up to bad endings, so many you don't even notice you're moving. So don't judge other people, especially your folks."

No one ever answers your questions. They just tell you what they've got ready inside their heads, answers they've used before, for themselves.

After the visit to the Upper Seven Aces I started feeling better. Not perfect, but almost up to snuff, as Linc would say. I still got the terrible feeling whenever I realized Sebastian could die any time and I wasn't doing anything to help him, that maybe I was waiting for my father to die. I'd hear the in and out of my own breathing and I'd understand I was listening for his to stop.

It's odd too, I kept remembering the storm, not after Sebastian got hurt but before. When you're caught in a whiteout, you're part of the weather. You see and feel everything. The wind. Those evergreens doing somersaults with every blast from the southeast. The snow, the way it covers it all so evenly, like time passing. Like the individual flakes have designated places to land, like the days of the week. Piling up, crusting, locking the minutes together. An inch, a hour, then two, and then more. The wind rounding, smoothing sharp edges, then smoothing out time again.

I had promised myself I wouldn't pray because I knew it wouldn't help. Because Sebastian wouldn't want me to, and it wouldn't make me feel any better. It seemed like I'd be taking the easy way out. I thought about what else I could do. How much Sebastian had liked books, how in the winter he could read the whole day. So I started reading for pleasure. The very hardest thing for me. That's right, for pleasure, I told myself. I'd never had a teacher who didn't comment how I was a slow reader. Or slow. One told Moonstar I was a functional illiterate. At supper one night I asked, "What is your most favorite of all your favorite books?" Moonstar went first. She couldn't stop with one, she told me nine, which I wrote down. Little stopped at six, and Sun at seven. And a girl who sat in front of me who was always reading library books on the sly had another six. No one could whittle it down to just one. For some reason, collecting those titles gave me hope for myself too. I started reading those books for Sebastian, page by page.

OPHIR FLAT

I watched Little while he watched Moonstar, and Sunflower watched me. Our mother was in love; that's what Sun thought. It was like she had no bones; her body was melting toward Charles Albert as they stood together after school outside the Ophir Flat Elementary office. He'd come to use the copying machine, he said. Little always carried least one of his cameras, and I was surprised he didn't whip one open and start snapping away at them. But he was more selective now; he photographed mostly animals these days, and even then he had to watch a subject a long, long time before he'd record it.

You never knew what Little was thinking, no comments from him, especially about our mother. It was like she was part of some experiment he was going to report on at the science fair, and he had to allow the participants to follow their own inclinations. Little at twelve looked a lot like Moonstar, same height, same blond hair and blue eyes, but more skinny, weedy. I was the only one with dark hair. Sun looked like her father, reddish hair and wide shoulders. I could always tell what she was thinking: "Slut," she muttered, holding onto the back pocket of my trousers like I might go over there. "Behave, Roscoe."

The September weather was still summertime warm here in Ophir Flat, afternoons mostly in the 80s; you could still swim. The blackberries were all picked, but the apples were just hard green knobs. The summer people, hippies and tourists were going home again, leaving Ophir Flat to 90 inches of rain and a couple feet of snow spread out over the autumn and winter. The businesses here—the gas station/store, the bar/restaurant, the general store, the bar/hotel and the bed and breakfast—were spread out on either side of the one blacktopped main street that ran a couple hundred yards. The firehouse, post office and Ophir Elementary were further out, along with the county road department office and the maintenance yard. The houses, some a hundred years old, were scattered, half hidden by fences, conifers, lilacs, climbing roses and apple trees. There were a couple of flat roof modulars, double wide, but with gabled roofs built over their tops for the snow. That was what was left of the town that in the 1930s had a population of over two thousand, back when gold mining and logging were going full blast. A full half of the houses and businesses had burned down since then. The joke at the volunteer fire department was *We'll save your lot.*

Maybe the tourists were thinning out, but not the communes. Charles Albert was a sack of shit in my book. I'd heard he'd been around for a while, a couple years anyhow, at The Community. Meditation center, retreat, ashram—the titles changed but it was always the same place, and he'd renamed it The Spiritual Community. His compound was on about 200 acres on a logged-off part of our ridge. He subscribed to a form of Buddhism, it said in the pamphlets he sent out. He didn't want to be called guru or teacher or master like some of them did. He was The Guide. He was supposed to have worked in a university on the east coast. You can't trust those people from back there: they come west and look at us like they know what we're thinking and it's all wrong.

Charles Albert was getting a following. Acolytes, Moonstar said, but Sun called them simpletons. The Guide was a clever son of a bitch: he put his followers to work clearing land and making firebreaks on subcontracts from the Forest Service: they didn't just sit around listening to him spout off. The ones too old for that were put to work weaving the Shaker rugs sold through his mail order service; Moonstar said she'd heard it was the most profitable enterprise in our part of the county. The kicker was these simpletons were paying The Guide upfront to spend a month with him at The Community. It makes you wonder about people, how flimsy they are put together, how fragile, that they have to search around for some belief or person that makes them think they aren't all on their own in this world.

After Labor Day Moonstar allowed our grandparents to take Little and Sunflower down to the VA hospital in Palo Alto to see Sebastian. It took a lot of talking to get Moonstar to agree to the three days; Grandmother must have phoned a dozen times over the summer. I didn't want to go. I couldn't. Our grandparents drove up in their RV, big as a bus, and parked it beside the house we'd rented. It was like old times in a way, having them in the mountains with us. Moonstar kept mum during the visit; she trusted Grandmother. She just ignored Grandfather. And Elmer hated Moonstar: you could feel it in a room, as sharp as a knife in your gut. I waved goodbye from the porch, relieved I wasn't going with them.

But it left Moonstar and me alone with each other, waiting for the other to blink first. This year at Ophir Flat she had to go to schools around the district as a resource teacher, and to a lot of meetings, so the three days Sun and Little were gone, I made supper.

She was always on diets, so I cooked the fattest food I could think of, so weighed down with calories you could hardly lift the plate. I'd look fat things up in the lists in her calorie books. Brownies for dessert, with a whole bag of chocolate chips in the mix and a couple of scoops of ice cream on top. "How was your day, Roscoe?" she'd ask, sitting down at the kitchen table. I'd give her my two words, "Fine, Mother." I'd have the table set, water glasses and wine bottle; she liked a glass of chardonnay after school. She worked hard; I'll give her that. Mashed potatoes and gravy, canned corn and thick pork chops. "How was your day, Moonstar?" I was attentive. She liked to talk, tell about the new improvements she was making in the curriculum. I'd listen patiently, paying attention, nodding, even a smile here and there.

She in turn would ask me what she always asked, "What are you reading now, Roscoe?"

In a foolish moment I had made a list of books I was going to read. *Gulliver's Travels*, I told her. Sun had recommended it. Moonstar looked puzzled. "About the midget Lilliputs that capture Gulliver."

She had a question but didn't ask it. I felt relieved. Her questions always called for too many answers. I read close, too, remembered a book for months later, to be ready for her. Later that night she added, "You know, Roscoe, Swift wrote more parts to that book, four more, I think. The abridged edition you have just includes the one about the Lilliputs. Check at the school library to see if I'm right."

We didn't have a TV, not allowed, so when she suggested a game of Scrabble because she was so good at it, I didn't want to play. "Let's play chess," I told her. She was good at chess too, but I stood a better chance there. She was good at everything. Beat me five games in a row. No one got a free pass in our family.

She yawned first and stood up to go to bed. When I did too, we were standing close but apart, and I noticed in the mirror I was taller than her now. "By the way, that was a wonderful dinner," she said, and she reached out and touched my shoulder before moving away. I hated it when she made me feel sad like that.

When Little and Sun returned they were full of news. "Sebastian can move by himself and he said my name four times in a row," Sun said. Little had taken photos of him and developed them at Grandfather's darkroom. I only looked at the first of the nine-by-twelve black and white photographs. Without his beard and dreadlocks, he looked too young to be the Sebastian I remembered. In the photo he was smiling. "He thought I was you, Roscoe. He kept saying your name," Little told me. "That friend of Grandmother's who works at the hospital said he's making great progress. Head trauma takes time; that's what Ms. Chester said."

Later Sun told me, "He drools, Roscoe; you have to wipe his mouth. Dad wears a bib when he eats. But you should see him in physical therapy: he swims by the hour." After that, I looked carefully through Little's stack of photos and felt sick. Sebastian's eyes weren't focused in a couple. There was saliva dripping off his lips. His hair had grown back in patches around the knots of scars. In one he wore a baseball hat too big for his head. Someone had posed him in his wheelchair with four drooping roses in his hand. The three of us were sitting on the front porch when I saw that one. "Why did you take these, you shithead?" I yelled at Little. Jumped to my feet. "Why couldn't you leave him alone?" I started ripping up the pictures. Little stood up and was going to say something. I was so pissed off I couldn't tear them right. "You open your mouth . . ." was far as I got before Sun was between us.

That night I started thinking about my father,

and the Thanksgiving when Moonstar had left me up there at the cabin to keep me out of trouble. I couldn't get him out of my head; it was the photographs, I think. The offhand conversations we'd have after supper, just the two of us in the cabin, a storm hitting against the walls, making the hanging pots rattle. One time we were both reading by lamplight from our stack of old newspapers. *The Mountain Messenger* always had a section, half the whole back page, called "A Hundred Years Ago," articles that had been printed in the paper in 1882. In the one I was reading, two miners recently arrived from Indiana had been trapped in a shaft cave-in, one injured and unable to move, with the water rising in the tunnel. The miner who wasn't hurt grabbed the gold they'd found and got out of the mine. The other, by luck, got out too and crawled twenty-three miles before he found help. When he recovered he looked up his partner Billy, carrying a shotgun. Billy explained that they had been friends for eighteen years and the fact that he'd got rattled by the cave-in and left him behind shouldn't matter. They shook hands. Then, when his friend turned his back, Billy stabbed him to death and claimed self-defense and got off.

I asked Sebastian what he thought about that. "First, gold makes people crazy. Gold is another word for greed. Second, you don't have what most people think of as friends, after a certain age," he told me. "After school or the Army, say. And that kind of shared experience wears off with time. Friend is the most misused word in the dictionary. You're alone in this world, Roscoe."

"What about your family?"

"Let me think about it," he said. When he said that it meant the end of the conversation or topic. But he surprised me later when we were stacking wood by saying, "You'll meet people you should listen to, Roscoe. The kind that will influence you. Good people you might want to emulate. They can be anybody. That's what I remember as important from when I was your age."

"Like who?"

"You'll know. You have to find your own."

Sometimes we were almost a happy family in those days working up to the winter. Especially when I could stop thinking about Sebastian. And sometimes I did. I'd catch myself wondering how he was doing up at the ridge, and then I'd remember I'd been with him during the whiteout that brought the limb from the cedar snag down on his head, that he was in the VA hospital in Palo Alto. I didn't allow myself to forget about Sebastian, but I didn't always remember.

Sun had said "Behave yourself" and I did, and that whole month was a tranquil time for us. Sebastian was getting better. Moonstar was more discreet—it was a word I'd heard her use for someone else. The Guide was in the picture, but not in the foreground. I'd catch him watching us out of the corner of my eye. The hot news on the ridge was they'd caught the leader at the other commune with an underage girl and had a warrant out for his arrest. The thing I didn't understand was that his group was sending him money while he was in hiding. The girl had been in my class. We never saw her again.

I didn't see myself as the man of the house or the big brother. I saw myself as a spectator. Moonstar called me that. "Roscoe, you're nothing but a spectator; you're not taking part in your own life." She wanted me to take music lessons. Sun played the cello and Little the trumpet. The rural schools in our district had federal money coming out of their ears for things like that, my mother said, because of the unemployment rate and the poverty level. In winter we were bused over to a Highway 80 ski resort on Fridays when there was enough snow. There were overnight trips to Sacramento and San Francisco to visit the museums. I went to those. But I refused to have anything to do with sports. I refused to play. I didn't go when Little pitched. Baseball was the most boring pastime ever invented. Not to Little, who would listen to whole games on the radio, check the newspaper for scores. I went to all Little's basketball games, though. Gymnasiums were wonderful places, like being inside a drum, the yelling echoing inside your head for hours after.

Sunflower was ten and most of the time acted more adult than a lot of grownups. Her teachers kept their distance because she was so smart and had taken it upon herself to know more than they did and bring them up to snuff when they fell behind. But she could still act like a little kid sometimes, which always came as a surprise. A stray dog followed us home from school one afternoon: we still walked home together, a holdover from the period when I'd done some stupid things, as Sun referred to my gas sniffing and glue huffing episodes. "Don't feed that dog," Little said — Sun and I were both weak-willed, he thought. "It's just going to follow us home." Sun gave the dog half her peanut butter sandwich and we had a pet. I filled a water bucket for it when we got home.

Moonstar was against dogs. I watched Sun turn herself into a little girl again without effort, "Please, Mama, please." She was five years old again. Tears. I looked on in amazement. "I'll take care of it, I promise, I promise. I'll train her." That's how we got Parsnip. The name was from her yellow white color. Parsnip was maybe three years old, mixed breed, and still thought of herself as a puppy. For a dog to last that long in the mountains, unless they were just house dogs, was unusual. Cougars liked dog meat better than fawn. Porcupines thought they were a joke, bears would swat their heads off, and some of the neighbors around us would shoot them for sport or run them down with their cars because they barked too much or shit in their yard. Sun kept Parsnip tied in our yard, and in the house at night. She slept on the foot of Sun's bed, and was under the table at every meal. She didn't obey anyone. That dog would get away and refuse to come back: Moonstar would have to drive around town with Sun yelling from the car window, "Parsnip! Here, Parsnip."

At school, because we were Moonstar's family, we stayed out of trouble—better to say maybe that Little and Sun were top students in the district and I stayed out of trouble. When everything was going right, we were like the families you read about in school books: hard times made you stronger; there might not be a happy ending but there was always hope, like in one family in a book on my list, where the young daughter lets a starving man drink milk from her breast. I thought about that a lot.

Many of the people around us were on welfare. They got food stamps, commodities, some kind of federal, state or county assistance. Those who worked commuted to the county seat or down below to one of the larger towns. When Moonstar was upset she called our ridge a rural slum, and "This fucking place" once, when she was really disgusted. Both Little and Sun got money from Social Security because Sebastian was disabled. I didn't get the money because Moonstar had never registered me as Sebastian's son. I didn't care if I got the money or not. I had my share of the summer's dredging gold, and I knew I could get as much cash as I wanted by going out into the woods later in the fall and pulling up a few plants from some grower's plot and selling the weed to a broker. I had a cache of nearly a thousand dollars. I didn't flash my money around, but I did buy myself an expensive spotter scope so I could watch the birds from farther away. Sun had given me a good pair of binoculars for my birthday. Sun was generous. Little kept track of every cent he had and was tighter than the bark on a tree when it came to money. When he wanted some new equipment he'd drop a lot of hints to Grandfather, mail him the pages from the catalogues, until Elmer produced the camera or whatever it was. If Little was Grandfather's favorite, Sun was Grandmother's. They'd meet and from the hugs and kisses you'd think they hadn't seen each other in a hundred years. At times I thought I was Moonstar's. She tried really hard to treat us all the same like she always said, but I'd get that feeling when our eyes would meet sometimes; it was like we were speaking to each other, convincing the other that everything was going to be all right.

Little had his new cameras at the ready all the time; two of them dangled off straps and swung around him like pets. He looked for subjects. Sun called them victims. I think he went after people with his camera to see how dumb they would react, that quick dab of lipstick, or his favorite, pushing their nose hair back up their nostrils. Little would let them primp and pose, but he only took the picture when he was ready. Sometimes I thought he'd select a subject just to see how they'd react. He was getting his photographs in both county newspapers, so he had no lack of folks wanting their photo taken. Moonstar was on a committee that had to report to the Board of Supervisors, so she took us with her to the county seat to the Board meetings. On the way, Moonstar would warn him, "No games, Little." He knew what she was talking about. He was supposed to sit with the newspaper reporters, if any showed up, who I felt should have been paid out of the general fund to be there because those meetings were so boring you could only hope for a lightning strike; I overheard the editor of the *Messenger* saying, "Take me, Lord, I'm ready," once as some blowhard went on and on. But I'd spot Little creeping up alongside a wall while one of the Supervisors was putting everyone to sleep, and the Supervisor would change as Little got closer, turn his or her best side to the camera, best posture, loudest voice, more teeth, as Little zeroed in. But he didn't always take the photo. He'd stop, and the speaker would go back to his ordinary self, and then Little would start moving forward again, closer.

When I started thinking about Sebastian and couldn't sleep, I'd try to grab onto a time when we all lived in the cabin up on the ridge, before Sebastian got hurt, before Moonstar began to teach, when we all were safe and I was happy. The one I liked best was a St. Patrick's Day. I liked to start out with that in my head, all five of us together at 6,040 feet, that picture. Moonstar claimed she was half Irish, but she would celebrate any day she could: holidays, birthdays, Ground Hog Day, Summer Solstice, even the first day of the month. It had been a mild winter, a layer of snow still on the ground, but with bare places where broken grass showed, and the boulders were all freed up, and the sun was out and had been in the sky for the last week. The sun could make Moonstar burst into song, and we could hear her singing as she cooked, the cabin door open.

The night before I had issued a challenge to Sebastian that his children wanted to do battle with him in the meadow at 1100 hours. The three of us were waiting when he ambled up. We had been practicing unarmed self-defense with him as long as I could remember. From the beginning, Sebastian made us take a contest seriously. I can't remember how old I was one time, but I wasn't trying very hard, skylarking, he called it, and he grabbed me by the legs and stuck my head in a snow bank. He didn't force us to practice: both Little and Sun had quit a couple times, sometimes for a month, even longer, and they'd bring out a book and read while he and

I went at it. But they couldn't help themselves and would always join in a free-for-all.

This time we had a strategy that I thought could not fail. All we had to do was get Sebastian off his feet — combined, we weighted more than he did by almost a hundred pounds — then hold on while he tried to counter. Moonstar came out to start the contest. She was wearing a sprig of pine needles in her hair for St. Patrick's Day. She was always so happy when the sun came out and winter was almost over. She hadn't been to town since November but was holding up well. We lined up five feet away, facing Sebastian, who was puffing on his pipe. Moonbeam raised both her arms and yelled, "Gird your loins, warriors and warriorettes." We were all laughing, and then Moonstar called out "Avanti!" and Little and Sun charged. Each grabbed a leg, and I was right behind them, running as fast as I could and I cannonballed Sebastian in the stomach. It was like running into a tree, but he went over backwards, and I got a headlock. Which he broke, so I slipped his arm back for a hammerlock. Sun and Little were each holding onto a leg. Sebastian was off balance and I was able to hold him in place with my weight for a short time. He didn't allow any knees, kicks, chokes or pressure holds when we practiced, so we all were limited in that respect, but you always have to assume your opponent is stronger than you, and we countered his strength with our weight.

We were on the ground in a patch of snow but none of us felt the cold. I was sweating. He shook Little loose and started rolling over and over to get us to let go. He flipped me off, and I tried a flying tackle which knocked him down again. Sun had held on and Little got his hold back. We rolled another twenty feet out of the snow into some grass. "Say uncle," Sun said. "You can't get away." Sebastian had lost his pipe and was out of breath but made a noise like he was laughing. With all my weight on his chest, he heaved up to a sitting position and then forward to his knees. Then we forced him back down, right on top of a hidden hill of red ants, the most ferocious insects in the forest. The ants swarmed us and started biting, they had teeth like a wolf, but none of us would let go. "Surrender," Little yelled. Sebastian rolled us off the anthill and got me under him. We all held on. The man would not quit.

Moonstar came outside to where we were in a tangle. "You've been at it for an hour now; I call it a tie." None of us would let go until she pulled Sun loose by the legs and then Little. Sebastian had to get up before I could move. I felt like a tree had been lifted off of me. We put on our shirts and I killed a bunch of ants on Sun's back and brushed the rest off. I found Sebastian's pipe. We all walked toward the cabin stiff and sore. Moonstar had brought the food outside to the picnic table. There was a jar of last spring's flowers, dried dollar plants. We were running out of grub but we always had canned spinach, which was Sebastian's favorite vegetable we bought by the case. So there was spinach pasta. Spinach frittata. Green tea. And green frosting on the white cake she baked for the occasion.

We waited for Moonstar's toast and raised our glasses of tea. "To Saint Patrick, who rid Ireland of all the snakes and sent them to America. My grandmother used to say that," she added. We were hungry but we didn't dig in right away. I felt like the March day had stopped, like we all were suspended in one of those glass paperweights you could pick up and look at whenever you wanted; there was a second as we waited where we were the only people in the forest, in California, in the world, and we soaked up that instant like we needed to store it like energy for later.

I'd noticed before how it's hardly ever the good times that come up in your head, always the bad ones. I promised myself I'd try to hold on to that Saint Patrick's Day.

WOLVERINES

Saturday morning Sunflower and I were on the porch watching Little move back and forth from the road to the house. He was scraping up a couple days' worth of dead squirrels and coming back with his shovel to drop them into a cardboard box. Moonstar was sitting in her rocker reading *The Messenger* slowly, as if she were memorizing each of the six pages. It was early October; the mountains were cooling off. The last of the black oak leaves were sailing past like yellow butterflies migrating south. The trees of heaven and buckeyes were a withered brown like big dead weeds, but the evergreens, the firs, cedars and pines which made up most of the forest, were still greener than green. This was the in-between weather time for the Sierras, quick storms, some thunder, some lightning strikes, but rain enough to put out the fires before they got a start. Rain drops as wet as a half a glass of water each, and the next day 81 degrees Fahrenheit.

Gray squirrels were about the dumbest mammal in the forest. They lurked along roads and when a car passed they made a dash to dive under the tires, stopped just short of getting crushed, then reconsidered, dashed again and died, crunched between the rubber and blacktop into flattened lumps of fur. Neither Sun nor I would think of asking, "Little, why are you collecting gray squirrel corpses?" He'd have the satisfaction of giving us that information when he was good and ready, the shithead. Moonstar put the paper down and looked over at the beer box of flattened squirrels. You could almost see her coming back to the porch from wherever she'd been while reading the paper. She made a point of treating Little the same as she did her other children. "Little, what are you doing?" she asked.

"Getting some bait for a trap, Mother."

This was unusual. Little was a vegetarian now and a Buddhist and would not eat anything with eyes or kill anything, even mosquitoes. As a teacher should, our mother waited for Little to go on. "This carrion will be my bait to get a photograph of a wolverine." I didn't allow my jaw to drop. Sunflower laughed. Little ignored her.

Moonstar thought the answer over. There probably hadn't been a verified sighting of a wolverine around here in a hundred years; everyone knew that. You had a better chance of seeing Bigfoot or the ghost of Juanita haunting the bridge at the county seat where she'd been lynched back during the Gold Rush. I knew in some places trappers killed wolverines for their pelts, but also to get rid of them because they robbed traps; pound for pound they were the most ferocious mammal in the forest. But not this forest. Not until you were in Canada or maybe Washington state would you see one, if you were lucky. I'd come upon a specimen once in the San Francisco Zoo, lying on the cement floor of its cage like it was a dead rug. It hadn't look like the killer of the forest.

I was the oldest, the future mountain man of the family, the one who knew the woods, knew the stories. Sebastian's stories, and all of Linc's too. But because Little was so smart, I had to approach the subject carefully. "Little, there are no wolverines in Tahoe National Forest."

"We'll see about that, Roscoe," he said.

That Saturday morning was the start of Little's wolverine quest, as Moonstar called it, though quest to keep his record perfect of always being right is what Sun and I said. All three of us followed him into the trees behind the house, deep enough in so Little felt it was safe to leave his camera and timer set up on his tripod without worrying that someone would come along and swipe his equipment. We didn't have to go very far. No one in town ever hunted anymore; the only reason people went into the forest now was to tend to their pot gardens. The dead gray squirrels were gone the next day, and Little grabbed the camera and came back to the house on the run to develop the film. It was feral cats. Next time it was ravens. Then a bobcat. Little wouldn't give up. Moonstar labeled it an obsession, and Sun and I sat back to enjoy watching the pursuit. This was highly unusual, Little playing the fool.

After a while Moonstar said I was teasing Little too much and told me to lay off: "Roscoe, enough." But I couldn't help myself. We would be walking along, anywhere, in town or in the woods, and I'd hear myself yell, "Over there, no, there, there, *Gulo gulo*, a skunk bear" — *Gulo* was a name for wolverines because they were gluttons and skunk bear another because they had a yellow stripe over their shoulders, although they could weigh 50 pounds. Little never thought it was funny. According to our mammal book, wolverines were so tough and mean they could chase a bear or a cougar off from their kill.

I wrote Sebastian down in Palo Alto at the VA hospital. "Little says he saw a wolverine on a jaunt we took to Jackson Meadows and thinks he can get a photo of it. I missed the sighting; I was busy catching a twenty-six inch rainbow. And why would he think they'd be around our place, in the back yard?

Remember that old trapper, Elton, I think his name was, you introduced me to a couple years back, had those stories about wolverines killing moose and bears in Canada? He was a friend of Linc's. Linc is fine, by the way; I walked over to the ridge last week. The owners of the Seven Aces just told him he was the best caretaker they'd ever had at the mine and gave him a 30 inch TV." I tried to make my letters interesting, going back over the past so Sebastian would be able to remember more. He was getting better.

Sunflower put in a note too. She wrote her father every week. Little sent some photos. Moonstar didn't have time.

Each small town along Highway 49 had its own scheme to get the tourists to stop and spend. Ours was apples, the tri-county Apple Festival, which drew tourists from all over California, according to the Highway 49 Association that sponsored the event. There were apple trees everywhere, in old abandoned orchards planted out on the ridges years ago when the mines were working, and in everyone's back yard in all the small towns, and people brought in pickup loads of fruit, looking forward to making some money from the flatlanders. THIRTY VARIETIES, ALL ORGANIC was in big red letters on the banner at the entrance. Lug boxes of apples were stacked six feet high. Apple pies, apple tarts, applesauce, apple fritters, apple strudel and apple cider all available to the unwary. It was only ten o'clock but the parking lots were full and cars were starting to line up on both sides of the road.

Sun and I were snickering, walking past all the food booths set up in the old Covered Bridge campground, checking things out. Sun stopped at a cider booth, got closer to watch two men tighten the spindle down on a wooden apple press, and then the juice poured out the bottom and started filling up a ten gallon crock. Four women wearing clothes like from the Gold Rush era were halving apples into buckets as fast as they could to make them easier to crush, big Grimes Goldens, Winesaps and Sheepnose, all the old varieties. We kept our interested faces on, watching the whole operation. The reason we thought the organic apple business was funny was because no one we knew had ever been able to stop the coddling moths from laying their eggs in the apple blossoms, which meant that when the fruit formed there was a worm in each apple. That cider was part worm juice. There was a joke in our family: "Never eat a mountain apple in the dark." We all took great pains to inspect our apples before taking a bite. I used my jackknife to cut off chunks, and as soon as I cut into a worm tunnel I'd toss the apple. It was only the commercial growers that sprayed enough to thwart the moth, and Moonstar said their apples tasted like chemicals. Little had done a science project on the life cycle of the coddling moth that won a prize at the Sierra/Plumas County Fair. One of the women recognized my sister because she asked, "Do you want a free sample, Sun?"

"No thank you, ma'am." Sun could be the most polite in the family when she wanted.

We continued on our tour of the festival, maybe thirty different booths. More and more people were coming into the grounds. There was a man sitting on a chair playing an accordion with two women singing alongside. A couple of mimes wearing miners' overalls, each with a pick and shovel. An acrobat walking on his hands. I caught a glimpse of Genevieve from my eighth grade class and waved, but I didn't think she saw me. A string quartet started playing. Sun stopped to listen; she played the cello. She had me laughing when she put a dollar bill in the open violin case for the musicians. If Little saw that, he'd faint; he was a cheapskate. He'd walked down with us; he was around here someplace. I was getting in the mood. Sun could always make me laugh, and now she was mimicking Moonstar to perfection. "Thank you, but I prefer not to make that choice at this time," she said when someone tried to sell her a slice of apple crumble cake. She had her strawberry blond hair in braids and looked younger than she was.

When we stopped to watch the three white limos from the ashram turn off the highway onto the access road to the Forest Service campground, I noticed the river was so low that we couldn't hear it at all. There was a kind of stir as the limos parked. Then I heard the shout, "It's John Wayne," and spotted Little in the crowd, his hands still cupped around his mouth. Little liked to announce all the religious CEOs like that at gatherings, especially the guru from the ashram, I'm not sure why. John Wayne was supposed to have invested in the Slapjack Mine a couple years back, but he'd never come up as far anyone knew. Excited tourists were moving toward the limos.

Out stepped the richest man in the tri-county area, short, potbellied, in his sixties, probably, with white hair and a beard that went down his chest like a bib, his face shiny and dark like a pecan shell. He wore a skimpy white cloth wrapped around his waist and up across his chest like scarf. Bare feet. His followers liked to kiss his feet after his talks, lining up like they were getting something for free. I saw him step in goat shit once before a lecture but that didn't stop his audience from kissing his little piggies later. He had his business manager and attorney with him this time, plus the usual dozen followers, who'd just started a humming kind of chant; they were the permanent staff and walked behind him a few paces. They wore white jumpsuits. When everyone's eyes were on him, the guru snapped his fingers and the chanting stopped.

The guru always had a big smile on his face like

he knew something you didn't. He shook hands with the sheriff first, then the rest of the officials that had shown up. "That greasy freak brings a lot of money into the county," a deputy sheriff said behind me. The ashram had averaged two hundred fifty students a month last summer, a lot of whom sneaked out to eat at the restaurants and stay at the motels when the skimpy grub and lack of showers and the mosquitoes got too much for them.

No free samples for the guru. He was making purchases at every booth, enough to fill the hands of most of his followers with cakes and pies. His business manager kept slapping bills on the counters as his attorney chatted away with a member of the county Board of Supervisors.

A booth run by a real estate agency was giving away plastic yardsticks with their name printed on the back. Sun and I went over and got ours. I recognized one of the women at the booth. She had come to our house in Ophir Flat a month ago asking for the address of our landlords: she knew we were renting. She'd said that now that they were getting older they might be thinking of selling the old family home. I'd put her off, but that night at supper I mentioned it to Moonstar. We were having split pea soup, and she put down her spoon. "Let's buy this place," she said.

We all gave this some thought. The three story house, five bedrooms, two bathrooms, was the very best place we'd ever lived in. A whole acre, lawns front and back, and a double garage. But the house was a hundred and one years old, too, with square nails popping out of the wood on the weathered south side, there was no cement foundation, and the wraparound porch sagged. Some of the windows didn't open and most of the doors didn't close easy. It needed paint inside and out.

"Let's vote on this," Sunflower said.

"Does this mean we stay here for always in

Ophir Flat?" Little wanted to know. "Let's look at this long term."

Moonstar ignored him and went over and got her address book from the desk drawer, then started dialing. We could hear the phone ringing. She looked over to us. "What do you say, Roscoe?"

I knew what she wanted me to say and I said it. "Buy the house."

Moonstar started talking then and we heard her say, "My family and I would like to purchase your property. You mentioned you'd like to sell the last time we talked." When the conversation was over, Moonstar came back and finished her soup. "That wasn't so hard, was it?" she said.

Sun and I stopped to watch at the dunk tank. People were lined up ten deep to take their chance at giving our District Supervisor a bath. That fat turd, as Linc always called him, was perched on a chair over a big tank of water with a stupid grin on his face. He won elections by so few votes there always had to be a recount or a run-off. You couldn't buy him, Moonstar had told us, but you could influence him, if you had a big enough family of voters. "We always seem to end up with people like that up here," she'd added. "This county is run by my former D students."

A woman was winding up to throw her three baseballs to dunk the Supervisor. Instead of aiming at the bull's-eye that would drop him into the tank, she threw at the screen protecting him. One ball hit exactly where his head was behind the screen, and he flinched. "Damn, that felt good," she told her friend.

Genevieve passed with another group of kids from school. We eyed each other. She had been sitting in the desk in front of me since she moved up here. We never spoke much outside the eighth grade classroom, but I wondered if she thought about me as much as I did her.

No one had managed to dunk the Supervisor yet, the target was pretty small, but the next thrower in line was the pitcher on the high school team. A small group of people gathered to encourage him. His very first ball dropped the man into the tank with a big splash. Dripping wet, he got back into the chair, trying to smile. The second ball dropped him back into the tank again. A big crowd of people had stopped to watch now. The Supervisor was slower this time, getting back into the chair. Someone yelled, "Come on, be a good sport; I'll vote for you this time for sure." People laughed. "Don't drown. Cold water's good for you." Third ball and he was back in the water. He climbed back out of the tank, and when someone made a big show of buying three more balls for the pitcher, the Supervisor stalked off.

Sun and I watched him, dripping wet, make his way through the crowd. Then I looked around for Little to see if he'd been watching too. He was over in a field outside the campground, down on his knees taking a photograph of something, another close up. I pointed him out to Sun and I started to walk on. But Sun was still watching Little, so I looked again. I saw he was still on his knees but his face was in the dirt. We both started running.

By the time we got there I could see the smaller rattler had stopped striking and was starting to slither away. I put my boot down on his head and grabbed his tail and pulled his head off. The bigger snake was still coiled by Little's head, shaking his rattles. I yanked Little back by his belt away from the snake, which tried to get away down a gopher hole. But I got a good grip on his tail and pulled the snake back out and swung him around and smashed his head against a tree.

Then everything stopped. Sun had Little on his back. Trickles of blood on his neck. Two fang holes. More blood on his arm. People were gathering around. Sun put her hand on his chest, and I could see her fingers go up and down from Little's heart, but his eyes were closed. He wasn't talking. A woman pushed through the crowd, knelt down, yelled, "Call 911, get an ambulance here. He's going into shock." She was unbuttoning Little's shirt. More spots of blood on his stomach.

It was like I was reading a book about what I was seeing, but the pages were turning too fast for me to understand the words. The meaning kept slipping away. I could hear the siren from the ambulance coming a long way off and then it was there. Little was being lifted on a gurney; they were putting a mask over his face and turning a knob on a green tank. The ambulance was gone again; the sound of the siren less and less. Someone handed me Little's cameras by the straps.

Sun grabbed my arm. "Come on," she said, and started running toward home. I still couldn't get it into my head what happened. Just that Little got bit by a couple of rattlesnakes and was on his way to the hospital. The woman who had called for 911 was a doctor, a dermatologist, she'd said. "He'll be all right with an antivenin shot," she'd told us. "It's not serious; no one dies from snake bites anymore. Don't worry."

When we got home Moonstar was sitting at the kitchen table grading papers. Sun had to catch her breath before she could tell what happened. I didn't try to speak. It was like I'd forgotten English. We collected Little's robe and slippers and the open book on his nightstand.

We were driving to town. I was sitting on the back seat and I wasn't worried. When we stopped at Miner's Hospital, they didn't know what we were talking about: Little hadn't been admitted there. Grass Valley, then. Moonstar was taking her time, not speeding; she was always a safe driver. Looking out the window I saw what a beautiful day it had turned out to be, the sun shining in the bright blue sky like it would be this way always. When we got to the new hospital in Grass Valley they were busy; there had been a three car accident and Emergency was backed up. We couldn't find anyone to ask. We followed Moonstar back outside the building to the front entrance, and she asked a woman behind the desk, "Which room is Little McAdams in? I'm his mother. It would be Elmer McAdams; Little is his nickname." The woman made a phone call and then another. "Will you excuse me?" the woman said and walked down a hallway. We stood at the counter waiting.

It seemed like a long time before she came back with a man wearing a Hawaiian shirt and a name tag who told us he was the ER physician. "Mrs. McAdams, please sit down over here. I'm very sorry to have to tell you that your son has passed. He died in the ambulance; cardiac arrest, and they couldn't bring him back. I'm very, very sorry." He was holding both of Moonstar's hands. "Everything that could be done was done, believe me. Could I phone someone for you, a clergyman?"

"We want to see Little," Sun yelled. Then again, even louder, and added, "Now."

"Just wait here moment, please."

He came back walking slow. "I'm afraid there's been some confusion because of the multiple car crashes. The hospital inadvertently released him to Gordon's. I'm sorry, but your son was taken with the other accident fatalities to Gordon's Funeral Home in Sacramento."

We got the address and went back to the car. No one said anything. Moonstar started driving the sixty miles to Sacramento. I couldn't think of the words, much less say them aloud, but I heard them inside in my head: LITTLE IS DEAD, LITTLE IS DEAD. No one spoke. It wasn't a long ride. Moonstar found the place, right off the highway. And we hurried in the front entrance, as if time was important.

"May I help you?" There was a man wearing a suit and tie behind the desk.

"Do you have Elmer McAdams here?" Sun asked. Moonstar was staring into space.

"Yes, we're waiting to hear from the McAdams family."

Moonstar spoke up, "I'm his mother." He wanted ID, and she showed him her driver's license.

"Thank you." He handed her a plastic envelope with Little's watch, wallet and his change that he kept in a green leather coin holder. He started talking to her in just above a whisper.

I wandered off from the voices, down the hallway and past an open door, a room full of coffins, then another, an office, and another. Little was lying on a table in that one. It wasn't like he was asleep, not with the swelling: his hand was three times the size; his neck had a big lump. I stepped closer. His shirt was dirty; he wouldn't like that. A shoe had come loose, and I retied the lace. I didn't feel sad, not anything. I tried. Dead. Forever. Always. It didn't work; it was like I had no feelings.

I went back to the office. Moonstar was saying in her calmest voice, "You want me to pay you eleven hundred forty-five dollars for moving my son from Grass Valley to Sacramento, a transfer I did not authorize?"

"That's the standard fee for transportation."

"But no one asked you to move him from the hospital."

"It's the usual procedure, Mrs. McAdams. When we can be of assistance, we're always there to help, and rural hospitals simply do not have the facilities or equipment to care for the remains of loved ones that we do."

Moonstar pulled out a credit card.

"I'm afraid we cannot accept checks or credit cards, Mrs. McAdams; it will have to be cash."

Moonstar said in her teacher voice, "You're

going to have to; I don't have that much money with me, and it's a Saturday."

Sun made a motion with her head and we went out to the hallway. I led her to where Little was. She tried to pat the dust off Little's shirt. Then Sun said, "Pick him, up, Roscoe," and I did and she led the way out the side door and we went out to the parking lot to our car. I lay Little on the back seat and made him comfortable. I knew what we had to do next. "Go get Moonstar, Sun," I told her as I got behind the wheel and started the car. Moonstar came out first, then Sun, running behind her with the envelope with Little's things, and they got in the front seat. I was backing out by the time the director came out the side door and started chasing after us, writing down our license number.

I took my time, like my mother taught me, went the back roads to Auburn instead of on the freeway, and then took all the shortcuts I knew. None of us said a word all the way up, not even when we passed the Covered Bridge campground. We were home before dark, and I parked the car in the garage. I carried Little to his bedroom, Moonstar spread out a quilt for him, and I lay him on that.

Sun was on the phone: I could hear her talking to Grandmother. I had thought of calling her, but I couldn't even form the words to make the suggestion. It came to me: now that we had Little, what were we going to do with him? We turned all the lights off as if we were waiting for something. I couldn't imagine what.

I watched everyone. There was no sign of grief from anyone until Grandfather went into the bedroom where Little was. He broke down, started crying, and the sound took over our house. After, we just sat in the kitchen, Moonstar, Sun and me, and our neighbor Mrs. Oliver, who was in her eighties and had come over to help. Two teacher friends of Moonstar's plus that asshole Charles Albert were coming and going. I took a walk when he came in again, down to the river. Got as close as I could to the water and started jumping from one boulder to another down at the bend, where they were the size of truck tires, where Little and I used to race. I went for a couple miles and sat down to rest. Watched some of the guru's people picking up driftwood from the river.

I didn't understand what I was thinking. That Little wasn't dead, that he would wake up. That Little was my responsibility; I should have been there and killed the snakes before he ever found them to photograph. That I should go with him wherever he was going, not leave him alone again.

It was almost dark when I went back to the house. It was too quiet. Grandfather was resting in my room; Grandmother was reading in the kitchen with Moonstar. When the doorbell rang, only Sun would go to the door to see who it was. Most people didn't come in but just handed Sun food they'd made. I'd read about that in books before, but in our house no one was eating anything. I went over and sat next to Grandmother. She took my hand. "Are we going to tell Sebastian?" I whispered.

"Not now," she said. "Maybe later."

Sun called me and I went to the front door. It was the guru from the ashram, and it was the first time I'd ever seen him up close that he wasn't smiling. He had an English accent like Benny Hill, the comic I used to watch on TV with Linc and Sebastian over at the Seven Aces. He put his hand on my shoulder. "I'm sorry for your loss, Mr. McAdams. If your family would wish to have a religious ceremony as we do on the Ganges in my own country, we would like to offer our services. We'd be honored to perform the funeral rites for your brother. We have been gathering wood for a pyre by the river, should you choose our assistance."

I couldn't think what to say. I was surprised he

remembered my name. I had helped him one time on the bridge leading into town. He'd got a flat tire, and his driver had jacked up the car, got the flat tire off and put the spare on, but then one of the helpers managed to knock the hubcap where they'd placed all the lug nuts off the bridge into the river. I was fly fishing and had watched the whole episode. They were just standing around, perplexed, so I yelled up, "Just take a lug nut off each of the other rims to replace the ones you lost. It'll get you to town." It was the guru himself who asked my name and thanked me before they drove off.

Sun spoke up. "We appreciate your offer, Mr. Gupta, but we've got permission from the cemetery board to bury Little here in town. We'd like to be able to visit him later. But I thank you for your kindness." The guru nodded and left.

It had been Charles Albert who'd gone to the Ophir Flat Cemetery Board and arranged for the burial. Found out you don't need to embalm, all the rest of it, and then hired a man for fifty dollars to dig the grave. We passed each other in the hallway and sat in the kitchen together, but I didn't say a word to Charles Albert, just pretended he wasn't there, and he returned the favor. Moonstar's lover. Her gentleman caller, as she put it.

I went into Little's bedroom to see him later that night. There were magazine pictures of wolverines tacked to the wall, plus one big 24-by-36 poster he must have sent for. Little kept insisting there were wolverines around our part of the forest, even though I'd talked to the game warden, Mr. Gable, who was a wildlife biologist, and he'd talked to Little. My brother listened, he trusted the warden's opinion, and Sun and I were on the porch listening too, but Little still ended the conversation with, "Males can range a thousand miles to mate, even from Canada, if necessary, Mr. Gable. Besides, I saw one. I know it was a wolverine, and I'll prove it."

He had on his best clothes now, what he wore when he was going to get some science award, the dark green sport coat with brass buttons and black trousers. I stood there, not as long as I planned, thinking what words were right to say goodbye. But when I heard myself say aloud, "Goddamn you, Little, you always knew better than anyone else," I had to leave.

Ken, who had the Oroflame mine, made the coffin out of seasoned incense cedar boards he'd got from Wayne down in Sleighville. Little didn't fill half that box, even after I put in his favorite camera and tripod, and a brass plaque from the Lion's Club for his speech. Both Moonstar and Sun put things in, too.

It was a gray afternoon: the clouds hung low in the sky, filling up the canyons and ravines. Then I realized it was smoke and guessed the guru was burning the pyre on the river, even without Little. Most of the people from town were at the cemetery, a lot from the places around, and all the kids from school. At the graveside that shithead Charles Albert said some words. I made myself not listen, and finally his mouth closed. Moonstar picked up a clod of dirt and dropped into the open grave. The sound echoed against the wooden coffin; I had to cover my ears again.

Our grandparents went home the next day, and two days after that Sun and Moonstar and I were back in school. All the kids knew Little, and most said how sorry they were. "Thank you," Sun would tell them. I kept my mouth shut. Genevieve, who sat in front of me because her last name was Mason, gave me a long hug in the hallway that first morning back, and I put my arms around her and didn't let go. I am holding Genevieve tight, I thought, just like I'd imagined myself doing so often. Her hair tickled my chin. She pulled away first. Neither of us said anything.

The three of us went to school during the day

and sat around in our own rooms at home at night. We'd forget to turn on the lights in the rest of the house. Forget to cook supper, which we'd all always liked to do, and end up eating cereal. No one, no one ever went into Little's room. A lot of his awards and photographs left the living room walls and ended up in the attic.

Moonstar hired Mrs. Oliver to clean house a couple days a week. She would bake bread on Mondays sometimes, and the house would fill with the yeasty smell coming from the oven. For some reason it made me think of my brother, the way he liked to put a slab of cold butter on fresh baked bread, so much it always ended up dripping down his fingers. None of us ate much of the bread, and Mrs. Oliver stopped baking.

Sun phoned Grandmother every Friday night at seven and talked for a while, then hung up, and there was no more sound in the house. No one acted sad. No one said his name. But it was as if we all had died with Little; we were all buried in our thoughts. As if our lives stopped in place when he left us.

One Saturday night at supper, Sun fried some trout we had in the freezer. We'd frozen them in water in half-gallon milk cartons, so they tasted fresh caught. She'd rolled them in corn meal and fried them in olive oil, the way we liked them, the platter piled high. I had caught them over in the middle fork of the Yuba. It's always kind of festive when you eat something you've caught and cooked yourself, but not this time. We had to force ourselves. "Is anyone ever going to say anything funny again?" Sun asked. "We're alive, even if Little isn't." Moonstar and I just looked at her. But it gave me an idea.

The second week in November a storm dropped almost two feet of snow on the town, and that meant five feet on the ridge. "Let's spend Thanksgiving at the cabin," I said. They just looked at me. "We can ski in; the county is plowing Henness Pass; we can get close." No one bothered to answer me. But I started getting ready, got our cross country skis out, greased our boots and the bindings on the snowshoes. When we went to town next I bought all the things Moonstar liked to cook on the woodstove: a roasting chicken, sweet potatoes, cans of spinach and pumpkin.

I'd talk it up at supper. "We can stop at the Studebaker and start it up. Charge the battery; it's been too long." They'd watch me. I couldn't help talking more and more about the trip. "We'll take Parsnip; give her a ride on the sled in the high country. Let her run free. Look how fat she's getting." But the more I talked, the less they liked the idea of going. I knew I was showing too much enthusiasm but I couldn't stop. I had been thinking about it for a time now, even before Little died—it had started after Sebastian got hurt—how much I disliked this world. Just getting up in the morning and shutting your eyes at night and doing the same thing the next day and the next forever. And in the end you end up dead anyway. I was tired of the whole rigmarole. It wasn't only because Little died. He might have been lucky, leaving when he did. Playing with snakes. Getting a rattler to pose. He might have done it on purpose for all I knew.

It was Moonstar that finally joined in with, "Let's go up to the cabin for Thanksgiving," like it was her idea. "It'll be fun." I didn't care why she'd changed her mind, but I'd noticed that Charles Albert didn't phone or come around anymore. That the last time I saw him, he was holding someone else's hand. I remembered Sebastian telling me something up at the cabin that last winter before he was hurt. Sometimes, once he got started, we'd talked for a long time: he'd tell stories and I'd ask questions I'd saved up. One of those times he said, "You're going to find out love doesn't have a long shelf life. When it goes over a certain date it weakens. And weakens again. The time line is different for everyone. And then it expires." There was a silence after that, where we both kept our thoughts to ourselves

The Wednesday before Thanksgiving was a minimum day, and Genevieve and I were walking home together after school. It's so much quieter after a snow: there are no bugs or bees, the birds move on, tourists stop driving up and down the roads, summer people disappear. Genevieve's family had been up here long enough for her to want to leave this place as soon as possible. Their dream had been a bed and breakfast, and they'd bought an old hotel and spent all their savings fixing it up. The father had been a Chicago stockbroker who had come west on a vacation and discovered the Sierras. The mother was a CPA. Two older sisters besides Genevieve had already left, and she was ready to leave herself as soon as they could sell their property. The B and B barely broke even in the summer; in the winter they went into the red, the way Genevieve put it, and she added, "People are such slobs." She was the only maid, once her sisters were gone. When she was pissed off at me, she'd call me mountain man: she knew how much I liked the Sierras.

I tried to explain once. "You're not seeing this place like I do. Imagine not growing up on a street in town or in a neighborhood in a city, and not behind a mailbox on a dirt road, on a farm or ranch, but in the middle of 1.5 million acres of forest. Green and more green. Trees beyond trees."

Genevieve didn't buy it. "If you've seen one tree, you've seen them all," she answered.

We got a ride up the road with the state hydrologist on his way to measure the early snow pack. He had a couple kids somewhere in school, and he and Moonstar talked the whole way about education. When he let us off, we were only a couple miles from the Studebaker. Parsnip turned out to be a winter dog: her big paws kept her from sinking too far in the soft snow, and she was picking up good sniffs, casting out ahead of us like she was on the hunt.

It was overcast but not too cold, 30 degrees maybe, with a good wind from the southeast. If I was lucky, it was going to snow. The pickup truck was safe in the open shed. Started right up on the first crank. The sound of the flathead six made me think of Sebastian, down in the VA hospital. He wasn't coming back. Little. The family was disintegrating. Sun was talking about leaving too, "This stupid school, in this stupid town," like Genevieve. Sun wanted to live with Grandmother in Sunnyvale. And now Moonstar. She'd surprised both of us last week. "I've been accepted in a doctoral program at Davis for next year. I don't know if I'll take it yet."

"Where would we live?" Sun asked.

"I said I'm not sure I'll take it, Sun."

"Hey, wait a minute." I tried to keep my voice calm, "We just bought a house, we still have our cabin up on the ridge, and we're leaving?"

They both just looked at me. Moonstar wouldn't answer.

Moon and Sun went ahead and I stuck around in the cab of the truck, letting the motor run. Thinking. By the time I got to the cabin, they had the place warmed up, fire going in the stove, and Sun had shoveled out the front door and a path all the way to the shop and woodshed.

I went through the holiday motions; so did Sun and Moonstar. We weren't cracking jokes yet, but we got past Thanksgiving. Toasted each other with a quart of beer Moon had found. In the silences sometimes we looked around like we hadn't been here before, like the cabin seemed strange, the kerosene lamps, the kettles on the woodstove, like this was an experiment and we had never lived like this once, without electricity and propane.

Friday I got up early, and it was snowing pretty good. Finally. I couldn't help it; I liked the snow. Each storm was different. Everyone always talked about the delicate and beautiful design of individual snowflakes and how intricate and original each one was, but for me it was the way the snow piled up, fused and locked together in long blankets and drifts. For Sebastian—I liked the way he said it, too—it was how the wind smoothed out the crust into waves of snow moving against the conifers. We used to talk about snow like it was a person.

"I'm going on a jaunt to the river," I said. Both looked up from their books and watched me put on my Icelandic sweater, sweatshirt, coat and hat, and pick up my snowshoes. I didn't meet their eyes. I couldn't risk a goodbye. The wind was blowing the flakes around like they had wings. There was a good crust and I didn't need the shoes at first. I grabbed a snow shovel and the 4 by 8 blue plastic tarp out of the shed.

I tried not to leave tracks, but the way the snow was falling they wouldn't show for long anyhow. About a mile from the cabin I started to dig my snow cave, just big enough so I could slide inside and then shovel the entrance closed. I threw the snow down the bank, spreading it out so no one would notice. It was going just like I planned. Exactly fifty-six minutes and I was wrapped in the tarp and snug in my cave.

I wasn't cold at first; in fact, I was too warm. I shouldn't have used the plastic tarp, but when they found me in the spring, I didn't want the field mice to be nesting in my clothes. Just a frozen stiff body was the way I pictured it, like the trout frozen in the milk carton. Dying from the cold would be a lot better than drowning, none of the struggling, though it would be much, much slower. Like going to sleep, though. I shut my eyes but I could hear the sound of my wristwatch ticking. I should have left it in the cabin. It was dark inside the cave and I couldn't hear the wind when I opened my eyes. No sound.

I must have fallen asleep, because when I woke up I had to pee. I worked my clothes open and unwrapped myself from the plastic tarp. I should have made the cave bigger. I must have fallen asleep again, because when I looked at my watch the date had changed; I'd been there for twelve hours. I got drowsy again and started to drift off. This time I wouldn't wake up, I thought. Time passes funny when you're buried like that; it's like it has nothing to do with you. You're unplugged from everything. Disconnected.

The next time I gave a glance at my watch, I'd been buried for twenty hours, almost. I should be dead. Dead. I should have taken off my boots and gloves. That was the one improvement I'd make, to speed things up. I wasn't cold, just numb. And I drifted off for the last time.

The next thing I knew Sunflower was slapping me awake and Parsnip was licking my face. The fucking dog had found me. Sun was hitting away and yelling at me, "You stupid asshole, Roscoe. I should just leave you here to freeze. We've been looking everywhere. Moonstar was ready to go back to town and alert the Search and Rescue. Don't you ever think of anyone but yourself?" She gave me a whack that split my lip and yelled, "What about us? What about us? How much more can we take?"

We sat around the cabin while I thawed out. I had explained to Sun I'd built the snow cave to see if they really worked and I didn't realize how much time had passed. She must have told Moonstar that, but no one believed me. I kept close to the firebox in the stove, trying not to shake, thinking about what

I had just done. How Sunflower had said, "What about us?" Sun was so pissed at me she wouldn't talk to me or even look in my direction. Tramping around in a storm looking for me: I hadn't meant for them to have to do that. I hadn't thought the ending out, didn't realize there was one for anyone else but me. I couldn't look at Moonstar any more; tears were coming down her cheeks. Sunflower was right; I was a stupid asshole.

Moonstar had got soaked looking for me; she'd skied all the way to the truck and back. Her wet clothes were hanging on nails around the stove, and she'd changed into one of her old long hippie dresses. She looked so young, like she did in the *National Geographic* photograph from when we lived in the yurt. It made me realize there was no going back to the way we were. The family was broken and there were no spare parts to fix it anymore. Sebastian was gone. Little. But it wasn't right for me to leave too. I had to stay now. I was going to have to stick around. Long enough to see what happened next, anyhow.

I turned fourteen in February. March came, April: just another month to go and I'd be out of Ophir Elementary School forever. The wet spring had brought the wildflowers out: California poppies first, covering the hilltops like a fall moon coming up, then the lupine, enough to reflect the blue sky. Flags in the shady places. I liked springtime flowers, a fitting ending for the winter.

I was driving the car, Moonstar let me do that sometimes now, with Moonstar beside me and Sun and Genevieve in the back seat. It was Sun's idea to give Genevieve a ride; they were both on the volley-ball team. We were on our way to a dance at the school. Moonstar was one of the chaperones. It was the first time I'd ever seen Genevieve uncomfortable: I couldn't tell if it was because Moonstar was a teacher or my mother. I caught glimpses of Moonstar sitting next to me, half listening to the girls, not joining in. She was musing.

I'd tried to apologize to her for all the dumb things I'd done, and especially at Thanksgiving, but it just made it worse. She knew what I was going to say before I could get out an "I'm sorry."

"You don't have to, Roscoe, you don't. Please. It'll just make it worse."

That stopped me. No words I could speak would make me feel better, anyway. But I had to try to make amends.

When I thought of Little now, I thought of the wolverine he was so sure he'd seen. I still didn't understand that. Why did he insist that the animal was around here? Why did he want to think that? How smart did you have to be, anyhow, to believe in wolverines? And why did I keep insisting there weren't any wolverines?

I danced with Genevieve first; she liked to fling herself about in some reckless way and I tried to keep up. Her family B and B hadn't sold, and her mother had had to get a job down below. I'd picked Genevieve a bouquet of wild flowers on the way home last week, and she'd kissed me, right in front of the store. She knew what I was looking at whenever she'd turn in her seat, her breasts resting on the edge of my desk.

I didn't have to dance with Sun; she had a few admirers now. She was so sure of herself. It was like she'd take Little's place, and in a way she had, as the smartest student in the district now. She hadn't gotten over what happened at Thanksgiving and still kept an eye on me like she was just waiting for me to screw up again.

They had turned off most of the lights in the gym for the dance, and it took me some time before I spotted Moonstar over by the water fountain, talking to the new science teacher. There was some old sixties music playing, something slow, and I went over. I was taller than Moonstar now by a full head. "May I have this dance, Ms. McAdams?" She laughed. "Come on, Mom, dance with me." After she stopped laughing she went on smiling.

I had confidence in myself as a dancer, though I knew I wasn't all that good. We moved around the wooden floor in a comfortable silence. She looked up at me with a little smile, and all at once I realized I was feeling—it came as a surprise—I realized I was feeling happy, dancing with my mother.

ABOUT THE AUTHOR

Ernest Finney writes stories and novels, mostly set in California, often in the San Francisco Bay area where he grew up or in the Central Valley or the Sierras. His short fiction has been included in a number of anthologies, among them *O. Henry Prize Stories*, where his story "Peacocks" received an O. Henry first prize, *Best of the West*, and *Best American Mystery Stories*. His books include four novels, *Winterchill*, *Lady With the Alligator Purse*, *Words of My Roaring*, and *California Time*, and three story collections: *Birds Landing*, *Flights in the Heavenlies*, and *Sequoia Gardens: California Stories*. He lives in Sierra County, California.